After The *Storm*

DAWSON CHRONICLES:

BOOK 2

Linda Bridey

First Printing, 2015

Dedication

This book is dedicated to all of my faithful readers, without whom I would be nothing. I thank you for the support, reviews, love, and friendship you have shown me as we have gone through this journey together. I am truly blessed to have such a wonderful readership.

Contents

Chapter One ... 1
Chapter Two ... 8
Chapter Three ... 20
Chapter Four ... 27
Chapter Five ... 35
Chapter Six ... 42
Chapter Seven ... 49
Chapter Eight ... 58
Chapter Nine ... 65
Chapter Ten ... 74
Chapter Eleven ... 81
Chapter Twelve ... 89
Chapter Thirteen ... 96
Chapter Fourteen ... 105
Chapter Fifteen ... 114
Chapter Sixteen ... 121
Chapter Seventeen ... 133
Chapter Eighteen ... 147
Chapter Nineteen ... 159
Epilogue ... 164
Bonus: The Courtship of Emily and Bobby ... 170
Connect With Linda ... 180
Linda's Other Books ... 181
Cast of Characters ... 183
About Linda Bridey ... 185

Chapter One

"Hey, Tim!" Steve McHale nudged Tim Dwyer with an elbow to attract his attention. "I'm talking to you."

"Hmm? What?" Tim asked, his eyes never leaving the captivating woman walking towards them on the street. "Good God, look at her. Have you ever seen a more gorgeous woman?"

Steve grinned. "She's a beauty, all right, but you know she has a reputation, right?"

Tim's heart beat faster in his chest as she drew closer. "I don't give a crap. I'm no saint, either. I'll see you later."

"Wait a minute! I'm trying to ask you about a deal on that imperfect Clydesdale you have for sale," Steve protested.

"Talk to Daddy about it. Those Clydesdales are his domain. See ya."

Steve let out a growl of frustration and walked in the opposite direction.

"Hello, Miss Keller," Tim said, smiling at the object of his desire.

Renee Keller smiled at Tim as he offered her an arm in a gentlemanly manner. She automatically linked hers through his. "Hello, Mr. Dwyer. How are you on this fine March afternoon?"

He looked down into her sparkling, dark eyes. "I'm better now that you're here," he said, turning her around towards the direction from which she'd just come. "You're not busy, are you? Good, because I need company while I eat some lunch. I'm starving."

Renee laughed. "I guess my errands can wait a while. It's my Wednesday off from work since I have to work on Saturday."

"Your dedication to your patients is admirable. I'm sure you brighten their days. You sure brighten mine," he said.

Renee always enjoyed Tim's friendly flirting. "Thank you, Timmy. You're so sweet."

Tim knew that she didn't take him seriously, but that was all right with him—for now. "I do try. Now, what strikes your fancy today? The Grady House, Delaney's, or the Sweet Spot? My treat."

"I can pay my own way, Tim," she said.

Tim liked that Renee was independent. He'd also found over the last several weeks that she was very intelligent and driven—things that he knew few people realized about her. She hid those qualities behind her flirty, fun personality.

"I know, but I invited you and the gentleman always pays. Call me old-fashioned, but that's the way Mama and Daddy raised me."

She smiled again and Tim desperately wanted to kiss her sweet-looking lips. "All right. I can tell that I'm not going to change your mind about it. The Sweet Spot. I have a craving for a strawberry milkshake and one of their Reuben sandwiches."

"The Sweet Spot it is," Tim said, walking again. "So, what were you up to?"

"Well, I want to make some more of those pillowcases for the hospital, so I was going to Elliot's to get more material now that I saved up some money again. I like to make bright colors to cheer the patients up a little. White is so plain and it depresses me. I'm also going to buy more material for a dress that I want to make."

"You're so kind to do that when you don't have to," Tim said, holding the door of the restaurant open for her. "I'd like to contribute some money for buying material, and don't say no."

He helped her out of her coat and almost groaned over the way her blouse and skirt emphasized her generous curves.

"I won't say no, and I thank you. Material is still so dear even though the war is over. Although you're not contributing to my personal material," she said as they went up to the counter.

Their friend and one of Tim's housemates out at the Dwyer estate, Randy Cooper, greeted them. His father, Chester Cooper, was the junior butler in the Dwyer household.

"There's trouble if I ever saw it," he said.

Tim didn't miss the appreciative way his green eyes traveled over Renee and his stomach clenched with jealously. "Hey, Randy," he said. "Renee would like a Rueben sandwich and a strawberry milkshake. I'll have a chicken salad sandwich and a chocolate milkshake."

"You got it," Randy said.

He gave Tim his total and the horse rancher paid him. They chose a booth and sat down.

"So how are things going with Brody?" Tim asked Renee. He didn't really want to talk about her going out with some other man, but it was the only way to keep tabs on the situation.

Renee shook her head, her dark brows knitting. "I don't know. It's strange. Whenever we run into each other, I get the feeling that he'd like to ask me out, but he doesn't. What am I doing wrong? I don't normally have this problem with men when I've made it clear that I'm interested in them."

If you made it clear to me, I'd snap you up in a heartbeat, Tim thought. "You're not doin' anything wrong. He's an idiot for not jumping on you." He laughed. "That didn't come out right."

She giggled. "That's ok. You know that nothing offends me. And I certainly wouldn't mind if he jumped me."

Her statement was hilarious despite the fact that it piqued his jealousy. Her irreverence was another thing he loved about Renee. He'd discovered that at his sister, Devon's, wedding in early February when they'd danced and sat together quite a bit. He'd never paid much attention to her before that, but he'd paid attention to her ever since that day.

"If I were you, I'd just be direct and ask him what's going on. Then you'd know and you could move on if he's not really interested, although I don't see why he wouldn't be," Tim said. "You have a lot to offer a man."

Randy brought their food over. "Bon appetite," he said, smiling. "Are you going to Wolf Point tonight, Tim?"

"Yeah. I'm planning on playing pool. You wanna go?" Tim responded.

Randy nodded. "What time are we leaving?"

"Seven."

"I'll be ready," Randy said. "I better get back to work."

"Ok. See you at home."

"Are you any closer to convincing your father to put in a billiard table?" Renee asked before biting into her sandwich.

Tim wondered how she ate everything so daintily. "No. He's afraid it'll be too noisy when the band is playing and he doesn't want to add on a separate room since the bouncers won't be able to see back there."

Renee said, "I can see his point. You don't want anyone beating someone over the head with a pool stick or anything."

Tim smiled. "Some people could use it. It might knock some sense into them."

"I doubt it," she said, chuckling. "Randy, tell Booker that this sandwich is delicious!" she called out.

"Will do!" Randy hollered back.

Tim took a gulp of milkshake and then asked, "Let me ask your opinion about something."

"Sure, sweetie," she said. "Shoot."

"Well, you know that a couple of government fellas have been after Daddy about running for congress."

"Yes, and I know you said that he won't do it."

"No. He loves being mayor, although he did talk about retiring again, but I don't think he's serious. Anyway, he doesn't want to run, but I'm thinking about running," Tim said.

Renee's eyes widened. "You are? Why?"

Tim's strong jaw clenched. "Maybe then I could help our Lakota gang—and other folks, too. It's terrible what other races have to go through. Not paid as much, people in the nicer neighborhoods won't rent or sell to them. They can't vote, and don't even get me started about the reservations."

"You have such a good heart, Tim Dwyer," Renee said. "I'd vote for you, if I could. You have no idea how angry it makes me feel that women can't vote. You just wait, though; we will, and I'm gonna help make it happen. I've already been sending letters to Washington and I've gotten a lot of the women around here to sign my petitions."

Tim nodded. "That's another thing I'd like to address. I know I'm forward thinking on all of this, but women have brains in their heads. They can make informed decisions. You're proof of that. Look at all of the things you help do. Not to mention those innovative schemes you come up with. Like the way you got Devon and Sawyer back together."

Renee let out a delighted laugh. "That was so much fun, and so was breaking your father out of jail so he could be in the Christmas play."

"I'd have liked to have been in on that," Tim said.

She put a hand on his forearm and his pulse jumped. "Now, Timmy, don't be sore about that. We had to be careful how many people were in on the plan. I promise to include you in the next crazy plan we have to execute."

He smiled to show that there were no hard feelings. "Ok. I'm gonna hold you to that. There're two things counting against me about running for office: my age and that I'm not married. They normally want family men to run."

Renee finished her sandwich, chewing thoughtfully. "Well, there's not much you can do about your age, but you're very intelligent, caring, committed, and social. You're also tall, dark, and handsome, which doesn't hurt at all. It should be easy to find a woman to marry."

"I appreciate that."

"You're welcome. When is Kyle coming home?"

Tim's younger brother, Kyle, had been drafted at the start of the Great War and hadn't yet returned home even though the war had ended in November the previous year. The military branches were sending the married men home first.

"I forgot to tell you—he's coming home this coming Monday. We're picking him up in Helena," he answered.

"That's wonderful! You must all be so happy that he's finally coming home!"

"We are. We've all missed him a lot. It was hard having him and Bobby in the war, but we're really proud of them," Tim said.

"As well you should be. I'm proud of them, too. They're such brave men," Renee said. "Mmm. That was so good. I'd better be on my way so I can get that material. I'd like to get some pillowcases done before I have to start dinner. It's my turn to cook tonight," she said.

She shared cooking duties with her father, Switch, when her mother, Hope, had to work late. Switch was working at Foster's Furniture with his long-time friend, Will Foster. Switch's position there was unusual. He was a talented actor and comedian and he performed skits and soliloquies for Will and Hawk, Will's business partner.

Switch's entertainment helped their work go better for whatever reason and he'd been doing it for a long time. He also worked a couple of nights a week as an orderly at the hospital where Hope was the administrator, in addition to taking a couple of overnight shifts a week on the telegraph machine and telephone switchboard.

Tim said, "What are you making?"

"Fried pork chops, mashed potatoes, creamed peas, and I made brownies this morning."

"I'll be over," Tim said.

Renee smiled. "I'll set a place for you."

"Oh, I was only kidding. I didn't mean to invite myself," Tim said.

"You're welcome anytime, Tim. We *are* friends, after all. Oh! I have a splendid idea! Bring Randy and then we can all go to Wolf Point together. Now who's inviting themselves?" she said with a wink.

Her idea appealed to him. "It's a deal. What time should we be there?"

"Five-thirty sharp. That way we can leave on time. Pa and Skip can do the dishes since I'll cook," she said, rising.

Tim got up with her. "I look forward to it. I'll let Randy know." He held her coat for her.

Renee rose up on tiptoe, giving his cheek a friendly peck. "See you then."

Her perfume stirred his desire for her and he could barely restrain himself from grabbing her and kissing her. He sighed as he watched her leave and then went to talk to Randy.

Chapter Two

As Kyle Dwyer traveled on the ship headed back to the United States that Wednesday, he had trouble quelling his impatience to get home. He hadn't laid eyes on his family since June of 1917 and he had a bad case of homesickness. It had been an eventful twenty months since leaving Dawson, Montana. That time had been fraught with heartache, laughs, danger, and excitement.

His mind wandered back to an unusual event that had occurred in the fall of last year that he would never forget:

October 27, 1918

Right before Halloween, Kyle sat in a trench, eagerly opening a letter from home.

Dear big brother,

I have a lot to tell you and I'm not kidding about any of it. I'm getting married on Thanksgiving.

Kyle's dark eyebrows rose. "Jr.'s getting married? Nah. Can't be." He continued reading Joey's account of his relationship with Snow Song and everything that had happened since they'd been found out. "Good Lord! I can just imagine Mama and Daddy's faces. Raven and Zoe's, too. Leave it up to Jr. to stir things up."

Art looked over at Kyle, "What are you mumbling about?"

"My little brother, Joey, is gettin' married on Thanksgiving. I wish I could be there, damn it. He's only seventeen," Kyle replied to the tall black man.

"Dang, that's young. What'd he do? Get some girl in the family way?" Art asked, smiling.

"Well, she ain't pregnant, but they've been carrying on. Seems like they're in love. He sounds really happy about it," Kyle said. "I know the girl he's marrying, too. She's really pretty and good with weapons, too."

"Is she one of those Lakota friends of yours?"

"Yeah. Too bad she ain't over here. She'd show up some of these fellas, especially with a bow and arrows," Kyle said. "The Hun wouldn't stand a chance against her. That Indian fella I told you about that I ran into a while back is her cousin."

Art stood up. "You sure know a lot of people. I'll take a look up top here."

"Be careful. It's been quiet for a while," Kyle said. "It feels like trouble is brewing."

As if on cue, cannon fire sounded followed by explosions not too far away.

"Told you," Kyle said, grinning up at the broad-shouldered colored man.

Art gave him a rude hand gesture and sat down just as someone landed in their trench. In that moment, Kyle received the shock of his life. The soldier stood up, brushing himself off a little.

"Nice of you to drop in, soldier," Kyle said. "How's it looking up there?"

The soldier looked at him, gray eyes wide and frightened, meeting his hazel gaze that immediately filled with disbelief.

After glancing quickly at Art, in a husky voice the soldier said, "As soon as they reload, we're moving forward, sir."

"Hailey?" Kyle said in disbelief as he looked her over. She wore a lance corporal uniform and a helmet.

"Kyle?"

He closed his eyes and shook his head, certain that he was having a hallucination. However, she was still there when he opened his eyes.

Art asked Kyle, "You know him?"

Hailey's eyes opened even wider and Kyle read the plea in them. "Uh, yeah. I can't believe you're here," he said tersely, the words having a hidden meaning he knew Hailey would catch.

"It's a long story, sir," she said, reverting back to her soldier role.

"I'll just bet it is," Kyle said. "What a small world. Art, I'd like you to meet my cousin, Hailey Dwyer." And I'd like to wring your neck, Hailey.

Art extended a hand to Hailey. "Well, how about that. He was just reading a letter from his brother. Good to meet you, Hailey."

Hailey took Art's hand, giving it a manly shake. Kyle had no idea what he was going to do. How had she entered into the fray without being caught? He remembered that she'd joined the Red Cross. How had she gotten from there to being in battle? Scrutinizing her again, he thought that it was a good thing that she was almost six feet tall and slim with it.

Her tunic hid a lot of her torso and the slight softness of her face could be explained by saying that she was only eighteen or nineteen, which she wasn't. She wasn't much younger than his twenty-four years. With a dirty face and hands, it was easy to see why she'd passed as a man thus far. But what happened when they left the front lines and went to shower? The men mostly showered together and there would be no hiding the fact that she was a woman.

Artillery shells landed nearby and Kyle's instinct was to throw himself over her, but it would look suspicious to Art. Hailey ducked as dirt and rocks rained down on them, but she didn't flinch. She smiled at Kyle and he realized that she was enjoying herself. It has to be her Lakota blood. Battle excites her. He had so many questions, but they couldn't be answered right then.

What was he going to do when they started moving forward? He couldn't let her fight, but he couldn't leave her behind, either. He gauged how much he could trust Art and how angry Hailey would be if he told Art her true identity. He had to get her to the rear or to the Red Cross. Wherever she'd come from, she had to go back there.

In Indian sign, he asked, "What are you doing here? Where did you get the uniform?"

Hailey replied in kind. "From a dead soldier who did not need it anymore. I was a medicine driver (this was as close to ambulance as the Lakota language came at the time) *and he was one of the men we were transporting. He looked close to my size and we were in a bad spot. I put it on and sent the other girl back with the men who had made it. Then I came to the front to fight."*

"You should not have done that! Women are not allowed in combat!" he signed emphatically.

Her eyes narrowed. "I know, and that is stupid. The Russians have women fighting for them, and some British women have joined other fighting forces, too. I am a good solider and I have counted much coup already."

"How long have you been out here?"

"Two weeks," she signed.

He gritted his teeth. "You are not properly trained and someone will discover you."

She arched a brow at him. "I am as well trained as you were when you got here. From what I understand, many of our soldiers had to be retrained by the French because they were not combat ready. I need no such training. I am an excellent shot and I am as skilled at hand-to-hand combat as most of the men here. I have ways of hiding my identity and I cut my hair short."

Kyle shook his head a little as he remembered her thick, reddish-brown tresses. "I am taking you back to the rear. You are going to get yourself killed."

Her gray eyes turned lighter with anger. "Why? Because I am a woman? If you say that, I will hit you."

"You would really hit a superior officer?" he asked.

"Yes. According to you, I am not a real soldier, so there would be nothing you could do about it," she said. "You must make a decision. Either I am a soldier or I am not."

Kyle didn't like being backed into a corner and he wasn't going to let her do it to him. Out loud, he said, "You're not. I'm taking you back."

"No!" she shouted. "You're not!"

Art had been watching them and he was confused. He could tell they'd been arguing in some sort of sign language, but he had no idea what they'd been saying.

Kyle said, "Art, I'm going to swear you to secrecy. Hailey is— "

Hailey slugged him hard and he fell back against the trench wall. "Shut up, Kyle!"

Art grew even more confused. "Hey, knock that off. He might be your cousin, but he's also your superior. You can't go around hitting superior officers."

Kyle said, "You hit me like that again and I'll hit back. Woman or no woman, Hailey."

Her fist clenched in rage. "Damn you!"

Art looked between the two of them. "Woman?"

Kyle said, "Yeah. Hailey's a girl."

"I hope you're kidding," Art said. "Women ain't allowed to fight."

She turned her angry gaze on him. "I'll fight any man who challenges me. I'm a better soldier than half of the men out here. My grandfather is a Lakota chief and I've been trained by the men in our family since I was little. Give me a gun, bow and arrow, or a knife and I'll show you just how lethal I am."

Art's expression showed his surprise. "Don't take this the wrong way, but you don't look like an Indian. You must be a half-breed. Me, too. What the heck are we gonna do with her?"

"I'm taking her to the rear and they can get her back to the Red Cross. That's how she got over here." He gave her a hard look. "Was that your plan all along?" As long as he'd known Hailey, she'd been wild and fierce, not easily swayed from doing what she wanted. It wouldn't surprise him if she'd been angry at not being able to enlist and had decided to sneak her way into the battle at the first chance she'd gotten.

"No, but when I saw an opportunity, I took it," she said. "This is where I want to be. Not back there with all of those silly women who constantly talk about this handsome soldier or that. This is where I can make a real difference. Not there."

She took off her helmet and wiped sweat from her brow. Kyle looked at her closely-shorn head and could have cried. Her wavy mane of deep auburn hair was gone, with only red-brown stubble adorning her head. Then she put the helmet back on, fastening it just as more cannon fire sounded.

"You're goin' back," Kyle shouted. "As soon as we move forward, I'm taking you to my lieutenant and he'll see that you're taken where you're supposed to be. And if you fight me on this, I'll just knock you out and carry you there. Understand? This isn't like at home when you're just sparring. This is life and death out here."

"I know that!" Hailey shouted back. "But I can fight. I've done just fine the last couple of weeks."

Kyle moved closer to her. "Hailey, there's another reason you can't be out here. It's a good thing you dropped down into our trench. A lot of these guys out here are missing women and some of them would take advantage of you if they found out you were a woman."

"Let them try and I'll make them sorry."

"You won't be able to fight off three or four of them," Kyle said. "You're going back."

Art said, "He's right, miss. I'm sorry, but you better do as he says."

She gave them withering looks. "You can both go to hell." She turned her back on them, stepping over to the small, wooden ladder and going up a step—just far enough to see out over the top of the trench. Things seemed to be quieting down.

Suddenly the order came to move out and Hailey was off like a shot. Kyle swore a blue streak as he followed her. He caught up to her, tackling her. "Oh, no, you don't. We don't have time for this! Come with me now!"

He hauled her up with him and she knew that it was useless to fight. He would surely tell someone to be on the lookout for her if she succeeded in escaping. Kyle forced her to run with him to where his superior, Lieutenant Asherman, stood.

He saluted Asherman. "Sir, permission to speak?"

"Go ahead, Dwyer," Asherman said, wondering why Kyle had such a tight hold on the soldier with him.

"This isn't one of our men. She's a woman and she needs to go back to the Red Cross. She was an ambulance driver and ran into some trouble. She put on a uniform to disguise herself. Take off your helmet," he instructed Hailey.

Hailey took it off and threw it angrily to the ground. "I thought you were my friend, Kyle."

"I am, but right now, I'm a soldier first and foremost and you being out there compromises us in a lot of ways. I'm sorry, Hailey, but this is for the best," Kyle said.

Asherman angrily asked, "How the hell did you get out onto the battlefield?"

Hailey said, "It doesn't matter. I'll go back quietly, like the good little girl you want me to be, Kyle, but I'll never forgive you for this. Never."

His eyes held true regret. "I'm sorry you feel that way. I really am."

Hailey strode away from them without saying anything and Kyle followed her. "Is that really how you wanna leave things between us, Hailey? I might die out here. I sure as heck don't want us to be angry with each other the last time we see each other."

She turned around abruptly. "Then you shouldn't have turned me in!"

"I had to!"

"Fine! Go back to fighting!" she said. "Be careful." She hugged him. "I don't want anything to happen to you, but I'm mad as hell at you. You'll just have to accept that. May the Great Spirit keep you safe."

He hugged her back briefly. "You be careful, too. And try to behave, ok?"

She pulled back from him. "I'll behave as I want to. That's the best I can do."

He laughed and shook his head before running off.

Asherman came over to her. "You do realize you're in a lot of trouble for impersonating a soldier, don't you?"

Hailey smiled at him. "I don't care; I'm sure the press will love my story. How a girl slipped into battle? They'll be really interested in that."

Asherman's blue eyes narrowed. "Are you threatening an army officer?"

"No. I'm just suggesting that you send me back to the Red Cross without punishment and I won't tell anyone how I duped several officers and a lot of

other men. I also won't tell them that I killed twenty-one Germans while I was a soldier for the past two weeks," she said. "And I certainly won't tell them how I dragged one of our soldiers to safety after he was wounded."

Asherman was shocked. "You're making that up."

"No, I'm not. I'm not gonna stand here trying to convince you, though. The Lakota don't lie. We're taught to always tell the truth."

"Funny. You don't look Indian."

"I'm half Lakota." Hailey didn't feel like giving more explanation than that. "Well, I'm sure you have more important things to do than talk to me. Like telling our boys what you want them to do on this next offensive."

Asherman was sorely aggravated by her belligerent attitude, but he was also curious about her. "So you really fought for two weeks and killed twenty-one Germans?"

"I don't know why you should be so surprised that a woman can do that. The Russians have a lot of women fighting for them. If they can do it, so can I," Hailey said. "Look, am I going back or not?"

Asherman said, "Just sit over there for now. I'll get Corporal Gaines to take you to the rear."

Hailey went over to where he'd indicated and sat down on the ground cross-legged. Asherman looked at her for a few moments before going to talk to his corporal.

Kyle smiled as he remembered Hailey telling him and Art about what had happened after he'd left her with Asherman. The woman was a firecracker and TNT combined. He wasn't the only one thinking about the strong-willed Hailey; his friend, Art Perrone, one of the few people who knew about Hailey's short career as a soldier, stood at the ship's railing, his mind drifting into the recent past.

December 20, 1918,

After receiving a stern reprimand from her superior, Hailey had been reassigned as an ambulance driver. Hailey drove wounded soldiers back from the front, humming as she pulled in to the unloading zone and cut the engine. It had finally sunk in to many that the fighting was really over after so many months at war.

She helped transfer patients to the hospital, joking with the five men, who thankfully weren't severely wounded. Only one of them had a gunshot wound to the leg. The others had broken bones.

One of them, a spunky nineteen-year-old, asked, "So where are you from, beautiful?"

"You can call me Dwyer and I'm from Montana," she said, grinning.

"Ok, Dwyer, I'm from California, but I could be persuaded to move to Montana." His blue eyes twinkled as he hobbled along on a pair of makeshift crutches.

She laughed. "Wow. Willing to move to see a redheaded Indian, huh?"

"Indian?" he asked. "You ain't no Indian."

"I sure am. Half Lakota," she said. "Still want to move to Montana?"

Revealing her lineage was usually an effective way to ward off unwanted advances because of the prejudice that existed towards Indians, even the ones serving in the war.

The young man wasn't sure what to say.

Hailey patted him on the shoulder. "That's ok, soldier. Have a nice life. Glad you made it."

Smiling to herself, she went back to her ambulance to clean the back just in case she got sent out again.

"Mmm mmm. There's that fierce warrior woman," said a male voice.

Turning around, she saw Art coming towards her. She couldn't hold back a grin. "Hey! You made it! Glad to see you. Are you hurt?"

"Shot in the foot," he said, smiling as he limped. "No, I didn't shoot myself, either. It'll be better before I'm married. So I see they didn't send you home or throw you in the hoosegow."

"Nah. I had 'em by the balls since I threatened to tell every newspaper about my story. Besides, they needed me. I convinced them to let me drive ambulance in exchange for my silence."

"That's good. Am I keepin' you?" he asked.

"Nope. I can talk while I clean," she said, gathering up her supplies. "Where's your partner in crime?"

"Your cousin? Around here somewhere. He came with me to get stitched up from some shrapnel." Seeing the instant concern on her face, he said, "He's ok. They got it out and it didn't hit anything vital. It was mainly on his back. He'll have some scars, but that'll give him something to talk about."

Hailey laughed. "He doesn't need any help in that department."

"No, he doesn't," Art agreed. "So when you're done here, can a soldier buy you a cup of coffee?"

She smiled. "Why, Art, are you asking me on a date?"

His dark eyes gleamed with amusement. "And what if I was?"

"I don't know. They say war romances don't work out," she joked, climbing up into the back of the ambulance to start wiping it out.

He chuckled as he moved closer so they could still talk. "Who said anything about romance? I'm just talking about a cup of coffee."

"Well, first it's a cup of coffee and the next thing you know, you're getting married."

Art laughed. "Boy, you sure are in a hurry, girl."

"Actually, marriage isn't on my dance card," Hailey said, ringing out her rag. "So where's home for you?"

"Well, see, there's this little place in Montana called Dawson and that's where I aim to go. Your bonehead cousin is dragging me home with him. Says he has a job for me."

"No kidding? Sounds like something he'd do."

"I did pull his bacon out of the fire, so he owes me," Art said. "Or so he says. I didn't bother correctin' him. He's been after me about it, but I didn't take him seriously at first. After the last letter I got from Mama, I made sure he meant it. Things in Louisiana aren't any good right now—not for my kind, anyhow. He said Dawson's a little different that way, so I thought why not give it a try. Can't be any worse than home."

"Just prepare yourself for his family. They're great folks and very respected, but they're rambunctious and they argue a lot, which is funny most of the time."

"That's what he said. So how about that cup of coffee?" Art asked.

"I thought I talked you out of that?" she teased.

"No, ma'am. You tried to talk me out of it, but I don't give up easy."

"I do like that in a man. Ok. One cup of coffee after I see Kyle," she said.

He smiled. "I'll wait and take you to him. He'll be happy to see you."

THE PRESENT

Art chuckled to himself as he remembered how the three of them had celebrated Christmas together along with some of the other soldiers and a few of the nurses. He'd noticed that Hailey hadn't been very chummy with the nurses and had remembered her remark about how silly she found some of them to be.

However, she'd fit in well with the soldiers, drinking, playing cards, and telling some raunchy jokes. The fellas had been enthralled by Hailey, who was beautiful despite her short, reddish hair. Art felt the stirrings of desire as he thought about her delicate ears and full, sensual mouth and how soft it had been when he'd kissed her at midnight on New Year's Eve at the impromptu dance at the hospital.

It had just been a friendly kiss and he wasn't the only man Hailey had kissed that night. They had been quick pecks of celebration, but he'd noticed the way some of the men had looked at her and he hadn't been able to blame them. After all, hadn't he noticed her beauty? The jealousy he'd seen on some of the nurses and nurses' aides' faces had been funny, too. Hailey didn't mind ruffling feathers no matter whose feathers they were.

A week later, he'd gotten to see her fighting skills when she'd taken down a solider who'd dared to put his hands on her rear end. By the time she'd been done with him, he'd lain on the ground, groaning in pain.

She'd looked around at the crowd gathered around. "Let that be a lesson to anyone else who wants to try getting fresh like that." Her gray eyes had flashed fire as she'd left the area and Art swore he'd lost his heart to her right then.

Kyle appeared at his side, snapping his mind back to the present.

"Some of the fellas are putting together a card game. You want in?" Kyle asked.

It would be a good way to pass the time, Art mused. He was as anxious as the rest of the men to get back to America. "Sure. Why not?"

He followed Kyle below decks, but his mind was still on the Lakota bravette with the auburn hair.

Chapter Three

Renee went to Elliot's after her lunch with Tim to pick up her material and a few things for supper. She hummed as she put this and that in her basket.

"Hello, Renee."

Renee stopped, turning around at the deep, male voice behind her. She almost dropped her basket when she recognized Brody Benson. "H-hello," she stammered.

"How are you?" he asked.

"Fine and you?"

"Good, thanks. You have a lot of stuff there. Do you need help carrying it?"

"That would be great. Thank you so much," she said, handing him some of the material.

"What are you doing with all of this material?" he asked.

She told him about her project for the hospital patients.

"That's really nice of you," he said. "Not a lot of people would think of doing something like that."

"Well, I hope someone might do something like that for me if I were sick," she said. She heard Tim's advice in her mind and stopped walking down the aisle. "Brody, are you interested in me? It seems as though you are, but you never ask me out. Am I imagining things?"

Brody blushed slightly and his blue eyes left hers for a moment. "No, you're not imagining things. I am interested, but … I don't quite know how to say this."

Renee smiled. "Just say it. I'm hard to offend, Brody. Go ahead."

"Ok. Your pa said that you weren't interested in dating and that he wouldn't tolerate any fooling around where you were concerned," Brody said.

A consummate actress, Renee hid her fury at her father behind a smile. "Oh, Pa is always kidding around. Don't pay any attention to what he said. I'm certainly interested, and I don't need his permission to see anyone."

Brody shifted his feet nervously. "No, he was dead serious. I'm sorry, Renee, but I'm friends with him, and I don't want any friction at work when he comes to perform."

He was one of the bouncers at the Watering Hole and Switch put on a show there a couple of nights a week.

"I see," Renee said, smiling tightly. "Well, it's nice that you respect his friendship. I'll take those now."

"I'll carry them for you."

"That's all right. I'm fine," she responded.

Reluctantly, Brody handed the material to her. "I'm sorry, Renee."

"That's ok, but it's your loss," she said, giving him a haughty look before sashaying away.

Brody looked heavenward and let out a sigh of frustration before continuing his shopping.

Renee fumed at her father as she walked towards home. She remembered that Tim and Randy were coming to supper and thought she'd better tell them not to since there was going to be a feud when she took Switch to task for his meddling. She turned at the corner and headed for the *Dawson Dialogue*, the town newspaper.

She could use the telephone there to call the Dwyer residence, one of the seven places around town that had phone service. Entering the office, she saw Chief Black Fox sitting at the telegraph machine taking down a telegram. He always took a shift on Wednesdays. She smiled at him when he looked up but didn't disturb him so that he didn't mess up the message.

It was amusing to see an Indian chief working a telegraph machine, but he was good at it and he liked seeing what was going on with the military forts close by and the sillier messages people sent to each other.

Renee set her things down on an empty table that was used for putting the newspapers together and picked up the telephone receiver. She kept ringing the appropriate extension until the Dwyers' head butler, Randall, answered.

"Hello, Dwyer residence," he said in his cultured British accent.

"Hello, Randall. This is Renee Keller. How are you?"

"I'm well, thank you. And yourself?"

She forced a note of cheerfulness into her voice. "I'm just fine. I was wondering if Timmy is home."

"Yes, Master Tim is in the parlor. I'll fetch him for you. One moment."

"Thank you, Randall."

The line was silent for several moments before Tim said, "Hi, Renee. What's going on?"

"I'm calling to tell you that it's not a good night for you and Randy to come to dinner. But will you still pick me up at seven like we planned?" she asked.

"Yeah, sure. Is everything ok?"

Renee blinked back tears. "Not really. It's going to be unpleasant at home this evening, I'm afraid, and I don't want you boys to get caught in the middle of it."

"Oh. I'm sorry to hear that. Is there anything I can do?"

"No, but thank you," she said. "I have to go now, but I'll see you tonight. Be prepared to buy me a couple of drinks, money bags."

His husky laugh in her ear had a comforting effect on her. "You got it. I'll take good care of you."

"I know you will. Goodbye, Timmy."

"See ya."

Renee hung up and saw Black Fox looking at her, his dark eyes filled with questions. "*Han*, Grandfather," she said, kissing his cheek.

He smiled. "*Hau*, granddaughter. What is wrong?"

"Nothing much. I'm going to kill my father, that's all," she said.

His eyebrows rose. He wasn't used to hearing people say that about Switch, who was sweet-natured and rarely had a bad word to say about anyone. "What did he do to make you so angry?"

"He's been interfering in my personal business. That's all I'll say for now, but I'm sure you'll hear all about it," she said.

"Be careful what you say, Renee," Black Fox said. "Words said in anger cannot be taken back."

"I'll try to remember that," she said, hugging the man who'd become a surrogate grandfather to her.

He chuckled. "I remember holding you as a baby. You were very cute."

"Was I?"

"Yes. You had such thick hair and it stood up like you were frightened," he said.

She laughed. "I'm glad it doesn't look like that now."

"No, it does not. You have become a very beautiful woman."

"Thank you, Grandfather. Well, I'm heading home. Have fun with your telegrams," she said, gathering up her packages again and leaving.

Switch whistled as he entered his home and hung up his coat and scarf in the foyer late that afternoon. Going into the parlor, he called out, "Anyone home?"

He heard someone on the stairs and went to the bottom. "Hello, daughter," he said, smiling. "How was your day off?"

"I had a very nice day. I made some brownies this morning and had lunch with Timmy," she said, reaching the foyer. "I went to Elliot's to get some material to make pillowcases with. I ran into Brody Benson and he told me something very peculiar."

He followed her into the kitchen, where she started peeling potatoes. "What did he tell you?"

"Well, he was somehow under the impression that I wasn't interested in seeing anyone. I don't know where he would get such a silly idea," she said.

Uh-oh, Switch thought. "I might have mentioned something like that to him. You haven't been out with anyone but Sawyer and that was just as friends. I thought maybe you'd gotten soured on men—"

"Stop lying!" she pounded the counter, making him jump. "He said that you basically warned him away. Why would you do that? It's none of your business!"

Switch dropped all pretenses. "Renee, it was for your own good. You're a very beautiful young woman and I see the way men look at you. You're my little girl and I'm not going to let anyone take advantage of you."

"Take advantage of me? Do I seem like the kind of girl who gets taken advantage of?" she asked.

An odd look flitted across his face. "Not exactly."

"What does that mean?"

His dark eyes sparked with irritation, a rare emotion for him, but he kept his words gentle. "Renee, I know that you, um, uh, *enjoy* men."

Deep embarrassment froze her in place and her hand clenched around the paring knife handle.

"I'm sorry, honey. I'm just trying to protect you," Switch said. "I know you're mad at me and that's ok, but please try to understand. I'm your father, and fathers protect their kids."

Renee laid the knife down on counter and wiped her hands on a towel. "I know you mean well, but have you done the same thing with Skip?"

"Well, no, but he's so shy around girls—"

"But if he wasn't? If he *enjoyed* girls, would you go around warning them away from him?" she asked.

"It's different for girls, Renee," he said.

"Well, not for this girl," she said, walking out of the kitchen.

"Where are you going?"

She mounted the stairs to the second story, Switch following her.

"I'm going to pack."

"Pack? Where are you going?" Switch asked, alarmed.

"I'm going to find my own place so that no one meddles in my business anymore," she said.

Switch put a hand on her arm. "You can't move out. Renee, don't do anything rash, honey."

She whirled around to face him when she reached the top of the stairs. "I can't I move out? Why? I make my own money, and I'm twenty now. If I were a man you wouldn't be telling me that. You didn't say that to Jethro when he moved to New York a few years ago. I never thought you were sexist, Pa, but I see that I was wrong about that."

"It's not like that," he said. "Don't leave. Where are you going to go?"

"I'll stay at the hotel until I find a place. I'm sure I can find a little apartment or something," she said. "Maybe move in with another woman who's in the same predicament I am."

"You call your father trying to protect you a predicament? You're lucky to have a father who gives a damn about you because mine sure didn't. You can be mad at me all you want, but what I did, I did out of love for you, not because I'm sexist," Switch said fervently.

Renee remembered her grandfather's words and reined in her anger as best she could. "I understand, but although your intentions are loving, they're still sexist. It's time for me to make my own way now and my own decisions. I love you, Pa, but I've made up my mind."

Switch fought back tears. "I can't tie you up or force you to stay, but please don't leave until you find a place. At least let your ma and me help you get set up somewhere. Please?"

Renee, like her brothers, adored her parents and her father's plea didn't fall on deaf ears. "Ok, Pa. Thank you."

"So, you don't have to pack tonight then," he said.

"No, but I do have to get ready to go out with Timmy and Randy," she said. "We're going over to the Howler in Wolf Point. They want to play pool."

Switch didn't like her going to the rowdy saloon, but he knew that Tim and Randy would take good care of her. "Ok."

"They'll be here at seven." She kissed his cheek and went to her room, shutting the door behind her.

Switch went back down the stairs slowly in a state of shock. Putting his scarf and coat back on, he headed out into the cold winter wind.

Chapter Four

When Tim pulled up to the Keller house in his Model T, Renee was waiting outside for him. Randy had sat in back so that Renee could sit next to Tim.

"Hi, fellas," she said, her expression bright. "I'm ready for a good time. How about you?"

"Yeah," Randy agreed. "I'm ready to make some money at pool."

Tim said, "Me, too. You can be our lady luck."

"I will certainly do that," she said as Tim pulled out.

Tim said, "I hope you weren't waiting long."

"Only a few minutes," Renee replied.

"Everything ok? I was a little worried after you called me," Tim said.

"Well, I had a pleasant argument with Pa, which is usually the way we fight, so I'm not sure if you can call it fighting. However, I had quite the row with Ma. Anyway, the windup is that I'm moving out."

Tim gave her a sharp look. "Moving out? It was that bad?"

"Yes, but I'd rather not talk about it, if that's ok?" she asked.

"Uh, sure, I guess," Randy said. "That's a pretty big deal, though, Renee."

She tossed her head a little. "Yes, it is, but this way people won't be able to stick their noses where they don't belong."

Tim was even more curious about what had happened, but her tense expression told him that she was very upset and he didn't want to keep asking her questions. Instead, he sought to ease her agitation by making her laugh.

"Guess what?"

"What?" she asked.

"Jasmine grounded Daddy and Joey," he said.

Randy laughed. "It was so funny."

"What happened?" Renee asked.

"Well, they were arguing because Joey jumped the fence with Fern, that new Thoroughbred we bought. Daddy saw him and about had a heart attack. So he was swearing a blue streak at Joey and Joey was yellin' back like he does. Jasmine walks right up to them and shouts, 'Hey! Shut up!' Well, they did. She points at Joey and says, 'You're grounded for a week for jumpin' that fence like that. You should have checked her a little sooner than you did before going over. No dessert at supper.' Then she points at Daddy and says, 'And no whiskey for you for a week for swearin' like that. I have spoken!'"

They all laughed for several minutes. "I have spoken" was a phrase that Black Fox often used when he was done reprimanding someone or giving them an order that he expected to be followed. Sometimes he meant it jokingly and other times he was dead serious. Jasmine, Tim's niece, had picked up the phrase from him.

"She's too much," Renee said. "Did they listen to her?"

Tim said, "Well, Jr. didn't have any pineapple upside-down cake at supper and Daddy didn't have his usual drink after supper, so I guess they did."

He and Randy kept talking about humorous subjects the whole way to Wolf Point and Renee was grateful to them for it. The Howler was crowded and Tim shouldered a path ahead of Renee to the bar.

Jinxy Jenkins, a petite blonde, smiled at them. "Well, there's one of those handsome Dwyer boys. Oh! And Randy, you sweet thing. Where's my kiss?"

Randy leaned over the bar and planted a big kiss on her cheek. "Don't let your man see that or he'll kill me," he said, grinning.

"Well, if I had a man, I wouldn't, but since I don't, there's nothing to worry about," she said, flashing her dimples at him.

"Yeah, but your pa won't like it," he said, moving back.

"He's not here tonight."

Randy frowned. "Who's helping you tonight? You can't keep up with all of this on your own."

"How would you like a job for the night? I pay real good," she replied.

Randy grinned. "I'd be honored to assist you, madam," he said, imitating his father, Chester's, English accent.

"Ooh! You keep talking like that and I might have to steal you away from the Sweet Spot," Jinxy said.

"Sorry, Tim," Randy said. "I can't turn down the kind of money I'll make tonight."

"Go ahead. Have fun," Tim said with a wink. "And pour us a couple of beers."

Randy trotted around behind the bar and put on an apron. "You got it. I better get a big tip, too."

Tim laughed and pulled out a twenty from his wallet. "Now, come here. If I'm gonna play Daddy, I have to do this right."

Randy set the beer on the bar for them and leaned closer.

Tim imitated his father's Texan accent. "Thanks for the beer, Randy," he said, tucking the money in Randy's shirt pocket. He patted it. "Keep up the good work."

Randy said, "Yes, sir. I will, sir."

Renee laughed at their clowning around and then she and Tim went to the back of the bar where the pool tables were located. Tim took her coat and hung it up with his on a peg on the wall. Then he sat down with her to wait until the current game of pool ended.

"Are you gonna play with me?" he asked her.

"Me? No. I don't play," she said.

"You don't? Wanna learn?"

She shook her head a little. "Don't you want a more challenging opponent?"

"I think teaching you would be fun."

"Why not? I'll try anything once," she said.

When it came their turn, Tim showed her how to rack the balls and break the triangle of orbs with the cue ball.

"Do you want the odd or even numbered balls?" Tim asked.

"Odd."

"Ok," he said and began to show her the proper cue stick techniques for whatever shot she was trying to accomplish.

"I'm never going to remember all of this," she said.

He put more chalk on the cue stick and handed it to her. She bent down, narrowing her eyes as she lined up her shot. "Five ball, side pocket," she said before sinking it in one shot.

Tim watched in amazement as she proceeded to make the next four shots in rapid succession. "You little minx! You know how to play."

"Oh, maybe just a little," she said, batting her eyelashes at him.

He laughed with delight, putting an arm around her shoulders. "You wanna have some real fun?"

"What did you have in mind?"

"See those two guys at the next table?"

"Mmm hmm."

Tim grinned. "I think it's time for them to lose some money."

Renee giggled. "I like the way you think, Timmy."

Three hours later, the three friends left the Howler, with Renee at the wheel since neither man was quite sober enough to drive. Although she loved having fun, Renee wasn't a big drinker and she was in complete control of her faculties.

Tim said, "Congratulations, Miss Keller, you made quite the haul tonight. Those boys won't forget you anytime soon."

"*We* made quite the haul, future Congressman Dwyer. I know exactly what I'm going to do with my share," she said.

"What's that?" Randy asked.

"Use it towards my new place," she said. "Wherever that will be. I'll have enough for my first month's rent and then some."

Tim said, "Will you let me donate to the cause? God knows I don't need the money."

"You're very sweet, Tim, but no. I need to do this on my own," she said. "Donate it to the Red Cross or the church if you don't want it."

"I'd rather donate it to you, but ok," Tim said, rolling down the window. "Lord, it was hot in there."

"Randy, how come you didn't ask Jinxy out?" Renee asked.

"Have you ever seen her father?"

"No."

"Picture a guy about the size of Raven who wears a gun and looks meaner than a snake. He's why I don't."

"So he's sexist, too," she said.

Tim heard the note of anger in her voice. "What do you mean?"

Her hands gripped the steering wheel tighter. "Why is it all right for fathers to tell their daughters who they can see, when they can see them, and expect them to stay virgins until they're married? Hmm? But why is it ok for boys to do whatever they please? Be with as many women as they want? Answer me that, boys."

Silence.

"You can't, can you? There's no good reason, is there? Just that it's the way it's always been. Well, you mark my words, gentlemen, that's gonna change and I'm gonna help it change," she said. "Maybe not this decade or the next, but someday, womankind's day will come and we'll be able to do whatever we want."

The fire in her eyes when she looked over at Tim was exhilarating and he wanted her to keep talking. "Like what?"

"Well, for starters, women will be able to go to college if they want to without a big fight. You told me just today that women have a brain in their heads and they should use them," Renee said.

"And I meant it, too."

"We need more men who think like you do, Timmy. Why are men so threatened by women?"

Randy laughed. "That's easy to answer. Because you're smarter than us. Other than brute strength and making babies, there's not much you need us for when you think about it."

Renee's pretty laughter filled the vehicle. "Oh, I love you, Randy. I don't know if we're smarter or not. Some people are smarter in general than others."

Randy shook his head. "No, you're smarter." He leaned into the front seat with them. "Ok, who usually ends up apologizing when a couple has a fight? The man. Why is that? Because unless a man is a lawyer, he can't think up a good way to prove he's right. And once a woman starts cryin', that's it. The guy loses automatically. That's not sexist, that's just the truth. A lot of guys can't stand seeing women cry."

He continued his observations, making them laugh. Their conversation remained lively the entire way home. Tim had Renee take him and Randy home since he wasn't sure either he or Randy were sobered up enough to drive. He would pick up his car from her the next day.

When they pulled up to the mansion, Tim said, "Go ahead, Randy. I'll be in."

"Goodnight, Renee. We'll have to do this again," Randy said.

"Goodnight," she said. "We sure will."

When Randy got out, Tim said, "Put on the parking brake."

She did, giving him a questioning look.

"Now, how about you tell me what happened tonight?"

Renee pursed her lips a moment. "Are there rumors going around town about me?"

Tim blew out a breath. "I've heard a couple, but you know how gossipy people are."

"Who have you heard them from?"

Tim didn't want to hurt her feelings, but he felt that she deserved the truth. "A couple of fellas were talking about you the one night at the Watering Hole."

Renee couldn't look at him. "And what did they say?"

"Renee, I don't want—"

"Please, Tim. Just tell me. I'm much stronger than you might think."

Tim said, "They didn't go into details; they just said that you're a little wild. Tell me what happened."

She looked straight ahead into the darkness beyond the windshield. "Pa has been warning men to stay away from me, telling them that I'm not interested in seeing anyone. That's why Brody won't ask me out. Pa told him to stay away from me, and Brody doesn't want to ruin his friendship with Pa."

Tim grimaced. "Ouch." Secretly he cheered Switch on, but he understood why Renee was upset.

"Yes. A big ouch. I don't want people interfering in my business like that. I know he meant well, but I'm old enough to make my own decisions. Brody said that he's interested in me, but he won't go against Pa."

Yes! Tim shouted internally. "Well, it seems to me that if a man is really interested, he'd figure out a way to court you and get along with your pa."

Renee glanced at him. "I'm glad you said that because I thought the same thing. If Brody wasn't man enough to stand up to Pa, then he's not the man for me. I mean, Pa's pretty easy to reason with most of the time. I've wasted months thinking about Brody."

Tim put a hand on her shoulder. "You need a real man, Renee. Someone who's not gonna let anyone come between you and who won't give up."

His voice held conviction and Renee looked into his eyes that gazed at her intently. He'd never looked at her like that before—the way a man looked at a woman he desired. "What are you saying?"

"I'm saying that you need a man who can appreciate a fine, beautiful, spirited, intelligent woman like yourself. Someone like me," Tim said, feeling reckless.

Renee's heart sped up as shock zinged through her, leaving her speechless.

Tim smiled, leaned towards her, and kissed her soft cheek. "I'll let you think about that. Be careful going home. I'll have Joey drop me off at your place on his way to school. Sweet dreams, honey."

He got out, gave the car a pat, and headed inside, leaving Renee to ponder what had just happened. She put the car in gear again and drove out onto the main road. She'd thought that Tim was just a friend, the same way Joey and Randy were. Tim's revelation was unsettling and she had no idea what to think about it. It kept her mind busy all the way home and when she lay down to sleep, her mind kept turning the situation over, making sleep impossible for a long time.

Chapter Five

"I can't believe she's really going to move out," Switch said to his best friend, Will Foster. "Was I so wrong?"

He sat in his rocking chair in Will's woodshop in back of the furniture store Will and his wife, Rachel, owned. Switch rarely sat normally in the chair. Right then, he sat with his back propped up against one arm with his long legs hanging over the opposite arm. Will had engraved Switch's name on the back of the chair and Switch absently traced the lettering with an index finger.

Will marked off a couple of measurements on a board before turning his green-eyed gaze on Switch. "Well, I'm not sure how to answer that. I can see why you've been concerned, but I'm not sure your methods were entirely correct."

Switch groaned. "It's hard when you hear things like that about your little girl and then you watch the way she looks at men and the way they look at her, Will. I'm just trying to protect her. I don't want anyone taking advantage of her."

Will's long-time friend and business partner, Hawk, said, "I feel the same way about Carissa. I don't think you were all that wrong. I've had to talk to a few young men myself about her. The only difference is that she knew I did it."

"Yeah, but you don't know Renee. She's rebellious in her own way. She's politely rebellious," Switch said. "She doesn't yell very much. Last night was the first night her and Hope have ever shouted at each other. It's the first time that I've ever shouted at either of them, too."

Will knew how much Switch was hurting over the situation. "Maybe she'll calm down about it and decide to stay. Give her a little time."

"That's not gonna happen, my friend," Switch said. He flipped upside down in the chair. "She means it. She talked about it at breakfast this morning."

Will smiled at the way Switch crossed his legs even as they draped over the back of the chair. "Well, kids do leave home, Switch. I can't believe that both of our girls are on their own now."

Hawk said, "And Jethro was about her age when he left home, and he went all the way to New York."

"I know, but it's different with girls."

The outside door of the woodshop opened and Tim Dwyer walked in. "Howdy, fellas."

They all greeted him.

"What brings you?" Will asked.

"Well, I came to talk to Switch. Do you have a few minutes?" Tim asked him.

Switch nimbly flipped right-side-up and felt pleasantly dizzy. "Yeah. What's on your mind?"

"Could we talk in private?" Tim asked.

"Uh, sure," Switch said.

Will said, "Why don't you use the storeroom? No one will bother you there."

"Good idea," Switch said, rising. "To the storeroom, my good man!"

Tim laughed at his theatrics and followed him to the room at the back of the shop.

"What's this about?" Switch asked, closing and locking the door behind them.

"Our families have been friends a long time," Tim began. "And we trust each other, right?"

Switch nodded. "Right."

"And you trust me, right?"

Switch smiled. "Of course, I do. Where's this going, Tim? Is everything ok?"

"Yeah. Everything is fine. I respect you, Switch. You've always been good to me, sort of like an uncle, I guess. What I'm getting at is that I'd never do anything to make you regret your trust in me," Tim said. "So that's why I'm coming to you about this."

"About what?"

"It's about Renee. You know we're friends, but what you don't know is that I'm attracted to her. I sort of let her know how I feel last night, but I haven't officially asked her out or anything because I wanted to talk to you first, man to man. Will you let me court her?"

Switch crossed his arms over his chest and regarded Tim with his brows drawn together. Tim had been out plenty of times with Renee and as far as he knew there hadn't been any hanky-panky between them. If he'd trusted Tim on those occasions, couldn't he trust Tim to court her?

"Are you in love with her? How long have you felt like this? What are your intentions? Have you kissed her? Done anything else with her? Because if you have—"

Tim held up at hand. "Switch, slow down. Look, I've heard the rumors about Renee, if that's what you're worried about, but not all rumors are true. You know that as well as I do. I haven't done anything more than kiss her on the cheek and hold her hand here and there; I swear. We've just been friends until last night.

"I became attracted to her at Sawyer's wedding. Before that, I didn't really know her, but we had such a good time that day, that I wanted to spend more time with her and I'm glad I did. She's beautiful, kind, funny, and much more intelligent than some people know. She's also strong, opinionated, and irreverent about some things, and I appreciate her for all of those qualities.

"I've never wanted to officially court anyone before, Switch, so that oughta tell you how much I think of your girl. I don't know what she'll say about all of this. I don't know that she'll ever think of me as more than a friend, but I'd like to find out. I promise to treat her with respect and do my best to make her happy. I don't know about love yet, but I sure do like her an awful lot. With all of that said, may I court Renee?"

Switch carefully weighed Tim's words. He respected Tim for coming to him this way and putting all of his cards on the table. Switch and Hope knew all of those things about their daughter, but to hear a potential beau appreciate Renee in such a way made Switch feel good. He'd never heard anything bad about Tim and he loved and respected the Dwyers, who had always been good to their family.

Switch's left eyebrow quirked up as he considered something else: if Renee was out with Tim, he knew that Tim would protect her from other men and keep her out of trouble—hopefully. The more he thought about it, the more he liked the idea of Tim courting Renee.

"Tim, if Renee is agreeable, I'd be delighted to have you court her. You're a good man and I have no doubt that you'll be good to her. Thanks for asking me. It means a lot that you did," Switch said.

They shook hands.

"Thanks, Switch. I promise to take good care of her," Tim said.

Switch patted his shoulder. "I know you will. Did she tell you that she's going to move out when she finds a place?"

"Yeah, she mentioned that," Tim said. "I know she was angry with you, but she really loves you and Hope. She's just grown up now, that's all. However, I will say this: if Brody was more of a man, he'd have come to you the same way I just did. I'm not saying he's not a good man, I'm just saying that he's not as interested in her as I am."

Switch laughed. "I agree. I expected more of an argument from him." He shrugged. "Oh, well. His loss—and her gain, as far as I'm concerned."

"I'm glad you think so. Well, I'll let you get back to work; I have to get home and do some work so Daddy doesn't chew me out," Tim said.

As he left the woodshop, elation filled Tim, making him grin as he got in his car and set out for home. Everything was up to Renee now. He decided not to go see her that day, knowing that she couldn't be pushed about things. It was far better to let her alone to think about the situation and come to him when she was ready. However, he was optimistic that luck would smile favorably upon him.

—∞—

On her lunch break, Renee sat down at a table in the little hospital cafeteria and prepared to eat her cold chicken sandwich. She was very confused over the situation with Tim. He'd never indicated before that he had romantic feelings for her. However, looking back, she saw that he'd been paying her a lot of attention ever since Sawyer and Devon's reception.

They had lunch and he took her out. He'd even had flowers delivered to her on her birthday. Weren't those all things a boyfriend would do for his girl? Normally Renee could read men very well, so why hadn't she picked up on his feelings? Maybe he was just that good at hiding them.

Why hadn't she thought of Tim in those terms before? He was a very handsome man with his dark brown hair and brown eyes. He resembled his mother, Lacey, more than he did Joe. He was tall, broad-shouldered, and strong. And he had a great smile, with a dimple in his right cheek.

Unlike other men, Tim had never pawed at her or treated her with anything but respect and affection. He always showed her a good time and insisted on paying for everything, which showed his good upbringing. Tim's sense of humor matched hers and he never made her feel like her opinion didn't matter because she was a woman. Just the opposite was true. He was always interested in what she thought and they discussed all sorts of serious subjects.

"You look deep in thought," said Dr. Marcus Samuels as he sat down across the table from her. "Mind if I sit with you?"

She smiled at the handsome man. "Of course not, Dr. Samuels. I'm always happy to have the company of such a fine-looking man. Not to mention smart."

His gray eyes crinkled attractively as he smiled. "Flirting will get you everywhere, but don't tell my wife."

"I won't if you don't," she teased. "You're a man."

He chuckled. "How nice of you to notice."

"A great man whom women notice, doctor. I've seen them."

Marcus put a hand to his chest. "I'm not surprised. I *am* quite a catch, you know. Handsome and smart, as you pointed out, and I do hold a prestigious position in town. I'm a good dancer and I can whistle, too. Need I go on?"

Renee laughed. "No, I think you covered everything. What I meant was that you can give me a man's point of view."

Marcus ate a spoonful of beef vegetable soup before responding. "What would you like to know?"

"Well, I've recently come to discover that a man whom I thought was just a friend thinks of me as more than that. I don't know what to do about it. It caught me off guard," she replied.

"Is he a good man?"

"A very good man. Kind, funny, thoughtful, and handsome, too," she said.

Marcus asked, "So what's the problem then? He sounds like a good catch. Does he have steady work? Is he responsible and honest?"

"Yes. He's all of those things. The thing is that I like having a male friend and I'm afraid if we explore a relationship, which I've never done before, that we'll destroy our friendship if it doesn't work out," she said.

"You've never been courted before? I know that's sort of become antiquated now. You've never seriously dated anyone?" he asked.

"No. I've been out with men, but nothing serious. I've never met anyone whom I liked well enough to see more than one or two times," she said. "And for the past few months, I've been interested in someone, but it turns out that he's been afraid to go against Pa's wishes regarding me."

Marcus smiled. "Switch objected to this man, I take it. God, I remember when he was just this gawky kid, and now he has grown kids."

"Yes, he objected and he's been warning men away from me. Apparently, I have quite the reputation around town, which I find odd since no one has ever said anything to me," she said. "I don't really give a damn except that it's prompted Pa to go behind my back."

"Well, fathers are like that with their little girls, Renee," Marcus said. "I was with Aiyana. When I caught her and Mason kissing, I was madder than heck and it took Black Fox to help convince me that Mason was worthy of her. Of course, it didn't hurt that Mason came to me and asked permission to court her. It makes a father respect a man if he's willing to do that. Are you attracted to this fella you're friends with?"

Renee finished her sandwich. "I might be. I should be. He's a virile, great-looking man. I just never thought about him like that; I don't know why."

"I'll tell you why, or rather, you just told me why. You wore blinders because you liked having him as a friend and you don't want the relationship to suffer. You must feel safe with him and have a good time with him. Now, he took the blinders off your eyes. You have to decide if you're willing to risk a chance at happiness or play it safe," Marcus said.

She pondered his words and then smiled at him. "You are very wise, Dr. Samuels. I see what you're saying. I knew that you could help me. Now, do you know of anyone who's renting a small apartment? I'd like my own place."

"You're moving out of home?" Marcus asked.

"Yes. I'm ready to be independent. It doesn't have to be overly fancy and I don't mind fixing it up. It'll be fun."

Marcus thought for a few moments. "Check with Sawyer. I think the apartment overtop of his shop is for rent, actually. I heard him mention it."

"That would be perfect as long as the rent is reasonable," she said. "I'll check with him this evening." She cleaned up her area and rose. "Thank you for the advice and for the lead on an apartment."

"You're welcome," Marcus said. "Always willing to help."

"And that's why everyone loves you so much," Renee said, squeezing his arm before leaving the cafeteria.

Chapter Six

Meeting Kyle's family the following Monday was an experience unlike Art had ever known. As soon as they stepped off the train in Helena, the Dwyer clan surrounded them, Lacey embracing Kyle tightly as she cried with joy over his safe return. Everyone else shed tears, too. Kyle laughed and blinked back tears as he was passed from one person to another.

It felt surreal to be among his family again and he tried to keep up with what everyone was telling him. It was impossible; finally, he said, "Hey! Slow down, everybody. I can't talk to you all at once."

Devon said, "We can't help it. We've just missed you so much."

He smiled at his little sister. "And I missed you, too. Now, let me introduce you to my good friend, Art Perrone. Art, these are my parents, Lacey and Joe."

Art had been expecting a cool reception despite what Kyle had told him. He was shocked when Lacey hugged him and Joe warmly shook his hand, clapping him on the shoulder.

"Art, it's a pleasure to meet you," Lacey said. "Thank you for keeping Kyle safe."

"We owe you, son," Joe said. "I don't know what sort of work you do, but there are a couple of different jobs you could work at if you want. We'll get into all that later, though."

The rest of the family was just as welcoming as they introduced themselves. Then the two men were borne to the Dwyer estate amid much laughter and conversation. Art thought, *it's like a party on wheels.* He'd never ridden in such a fancy car as the Brougham and marveled at its leather interior and shiny black paint job.

There were more surprises in store for him. When they arrived at the estate, his eyes grew huge when he saw the sprawling mansion and huge white barns with black trim. They'd recently been painted to match the house and their appearance was pristine and impressive.

Kyle grinned at Art's awed expression. "You thought I was lyin', didn't you?" he asked.

"Not lyin', but I thought you might be stretchin' the truth," Art admitted.

"Nope," Kyle said as they pulled up in front of the house.

Joe said, "C'mon, boys. Cora and Lucy are cooking dinner and you don't wanna keep them waitin' it on you. They get a little cranky about that."

Kyle said, "I don't think they'll get cranky today, Daddy."

"I expect you're right," Joe said, giving him another sideways hug.

The front door opened and more people spilled out of the house. Art was surprised to see a tall, buxom, older black woman grab Kyle, holding him tightly while he kissed her and returned her embrace wholeheartedly.

Art was introduced again; the men shook hands with him and a couple of the women hugged him. He didn't know what to make of it all. A little girl named Jasmine took his hand and led him inside.

"You can sit by me at dinner," she informed him. "I'll show you my ferret, Percy, later. You'll like him."

He smiled at her. "I can, huh? All right. I never turn down an invite from a pretty lady."

"Smart man," she said, making him laugh.

The house was as impressive inside as outside and Art looked around with wonder at the marble-floored foyer and parlor. He noticed that there were quite a few Indian accents around the place and thought that Kyle hadn't stretched the truth about that, either. He'd noticed Joey's wife, Snow Song, and could tell that the beautiful young woman was part Lakota. Other than the shape of her face, she didn't resemble Hailey much, though.

Art wondered if Hailey would show up. She'd left Europe before he and Kyle had, so he knew she was home by now. He felt an arm slip through his and looked down at Lacey.

"Now, Art, you come with me. I'll show you to your room and you can change and freshen up there," she said.

Kyle hadn't mentioned that he'd be staying in the house. "Oh, no, ma'am. A bunkhouse or the barn would be just fine."

"Nonsense," Lacey said. "You're our guest and we don't put our guests in the bunkhouses or barn unless we're having a party and there's not enough room in the house for everyone to stay over. Come with me."

He didn't argue as she led him down a long hallway and turned left into another long hallway. She stopped midway down and opened a door. "Here you go. There's a bathhouse right through that door over there and a washroom in the room right over here."

Art just knew he was going to get lost in a house this big. "Yes, ma'am. Thank you."

"Come on out whenever you're ready," she said.

Chester came down the hall with Art's duffel bag. "I believe this is yours, sir," he said.

Art almost looked around to see to whom Chester was speaking. No English butler had ever called him "sir." He took the bag. "Thanks. Much obliged."

"You're quite welcome. It's good to have you with us, Mr. Perrone."

"Oh, just call me Art."

Chester smiled. "Then you must call me Chester."

Art returned his smile. "Ok. I'll do that."

Chester bowed a little and left them.

"Art, if there's anything you need, just ask. You're among friends here," she said, her meaning plain to him.

Deeply touched, Art said, "Thank you for everything, Mrs. Dwyer."

"You might not be thanking us for long," she said, her eyes twinkling. "We're a rowdy bunch. I'll leave you to it. See you at dinner."

"Yes, ma'am."

As Art closed the door to his room, he felt like he'd stepped into an alternate universe as he looked at the fine furniture and paintings. He gathered up clean clothes and found the washroom. Once he'd cleaned up and changed, he put his clothes in the hamper he found in his room and went out to the dining room.

Cora, Lucy, and a few other people were helping bring food to the table.

"Can I help with anything?" he asked Cora.

"No, sir. You're a guest of honor. Go on and sit down," she said.

Kyle came into the dining room. "Don't argue with her, Art. She's tougher than any drill sergeant and she'll withhold pie if you don't listen to her. You don't want that."

Art smiled. "I'll remember that."

Jasmine patted the chair next to her. "Art, you promised you'd sit with me."

"Yes, I did and I always keep my promises," he said, sitting down.

Art's gaze roamed over the people who gathered around the table and marveled at seeing whites, coloreds, and Indians all sitting together. Not to mention that many of the people there were employees who were treated like family. It was a strange, wonderful place and Art was glad to be a part of it.

The next day, Renee looked around the little apartment over Sawyer's shop. He'd come upstairs with her to inspect it, too. Although he trusted the woman who owned the building, he still wanted to make sure the place was in good shape.

"All of the windows are intact and none of the floorboards are warped," he said as he walked through the small parlor into the bedroom. "There's even a decent closet in here."

She joined him. "Yes. You're right. I don't like these pink walls, but I can paint them."

"Actually, I think they were some sort of orange at some point, but it looks like it faded."

Renee made a face. "That's even worse. Maybe a light green or a cream color. Then I could change drapes whenever I wanted."

"Good idea. You better make up your mind quick. There've been a lot of people looking at it. Mrs. Bissinger will rent it to whoever gives her the money first," Sawyer said.

Renee liked the apartment with the eat-in kitchen. It also had a nice little pantry and several cupboards. Eleven dollars a month wasn't terribly expensive and she knew that she could swing it, especially if she picked up an odd job somewhere. She calculated the funds at her disposal.

Between her paycheck and the money she'd made playing pool, she had enough for the first month's rent and she was sure that she could pick up some secondhand furniture. At least enough for a bed and dresser.

"I'll take it. Let's go tell her," she said.

Sawyer smiled at the excited light in her eyes. "Great! Now I can bug you on your days off and when I'm working late on developing pictures."

She let out a happy little squeal and they left the apartment. Mrs. Bissinger waited for them downstairs in Sawyer's photography studio.

"Mrs. Bissinger, it's a lovely place and I've decided to take it," Renee said.

The middle-aged woman's eyes lit up. "Wonderful!"

Renee counted out eleven dollars. "Here you are," she said, handing it over.

"Very good. Let me write you a receipt," Mrs. Bissinger said. "Here are the keys and you can go ahead and move in whenever you want. This will be for April's rent. There's only a few days left in this month. I'm just glad it won't be empty anymore."

"Thank you so much," Renee said.

"You're welcome. Well, good day to you both and enjoy your apartment," Mrs. Bissinger said.

Once she left, Renee danced around gleefully. "My first apartment! I can't believe it. I owe Marcus! And you for putting in a good word for me." She hugged Sawyer. "I have to get some furniture."

Sawyer grinned as she rattled off all of the things she wanted. "Hang on, Renee. I can help you with a few of those things. I think Mama and Pa have some furniture in the attic at their place that you could have."

"I'll pay them for it," Renee said. "I don't expect handouts."

"You'll have to talk to them about that part, but I'll bet a lot of people you know have good furniture they're willing to part with," Sawyer said. "Devon and I are going out there for supper tonight. I'll ask them for you, ok?"

"You are such a sweet man and a good friend. I have to get back to work. I don't want to be late getting back from lunch," Renee said. She never took advantage of the fact that her mother was the administrator of the hospital. When she was at work, she was just another employee and she didn't expect special treatment. "I'll stop by on lunch tomorrow to see what they say, ok?"

"Sounds good," Sawyer said.

"Ta ta," she said, leaving his shop.

Sawyer chuckled and went back to work.

Polly, the nurse on the desk that afternoon, found Renee cleaning the room of a patient who'd just gone home.

"Well, Miss Renee, you have one heck of an admirer," she said.

"What do you mean?" Renee asked as she finished making the bed.

Polly looked at the colorful pillowcase on the bed and smiled. "They really do look cheery."

"Thank you. There's enough stark white in here. We need to warm it up a bit. Anyway, what were you saying about an admirer?" Renee said, brushing a lock of dark hair from her forehead.

"Come out to the desk and see," Polly said.

Renee gasped when she saw the dozen red roses in a vase sitting on the desk. "They're for me?"

"That's what the delivery man said. Read the card before I die of curiosity!"

Renee giggled and plucked the card from among the beautiful arrangement.

Your presence is requested at 7 p.m. this evening at Delaney's for a celebratory dinner.

Fondly, T.D.

Renee laughed. "They're from Timmy. He wants to have dinner tonight."

"My goodness!" Polly said. "That's some invitation. I thought you were just friends."

Renee frowned a little. "We are. I think. I don't know."

Polly gave her a knowing look. "A man doesn't send red roses when he's just a friend."

"It's a little muddled right now," Renee said with a fluttering hand gesture. "We'll see. Don't say anything."

"When have I ever betrayed your confidence?" Polly responded.

"Thanks, Polly. I'll go put these in Ma's office so they're out of your way," Renee said, hurrying off.

Chapter Seven

Tim waited outside of Delancy's for Renee, anticipation at seeing her again making him antsy. He hadn't talked to her since they'd gone to the Howler and he was anxious about her reaction to his remarks. Then he saw her striding in his direction and he was mesmerized by her. He walked towards her, smiling.

"Fancy meeting you here, Miss Keller," he said.

She took the arm he offered her. "Yes, what a strange coincidence. I received a gorgeous arrangement of roses from someone with the initials of T.D. I can't imagine who that would be, can you?"

"Doesn't ring a bell, but as long as you're here, will you do me the honor of dining with me?" he asked, glad to see that she was as playful with him as usual.

He opened the door for her and they entered the restaurant. She removed her coat, revealing a sapphire-blue dress that molded to her hourglass figure. Tim looked at her so intently that he kept missing the hook on the coatrack as he tried to hang up her coat. Finally, he paid attention to what he was doing and succeeded.

They chose a table and he seated her.

"I understand that congratulations are in order," Tim said. "I heard that you found an apartment."

"You must have talked to Sawyer," she said, taking in how handsome he was in his black suit. He was freshly shaven and his hair was nicely styled.

"Yeah. I stopped in to see if he had some pictures developed that I had him to take," Tim said. "You look stunning, Renee."

Normally, she took compliments like that in stride, but for some reason, Tim's flattering remark made her blush a little. "Thank you. And you look dashing."

He grinned. "Thanks. I'm glad you approve."

"I certainly do. How is Kyle? I'm sure you're all so glad to have him home," she said.

"We are and he's all in one piece. He's happy to be home, of course, but I think it's gonna take him a little time to get used to everything again. He said he didn't sleep much last night," Tim said.

"It has to be hard," Renee said. "He's used to artillery fire all around him and sleeping in a trench and eating meat from a can. It's going to take some adjustment. But with all of his family and friends helping him, he'll be all right."

Their waitress arrived and they gave her their order.

"You should come see him tomorrow night. He'll be glad to see you and you can meet Art," Tim said. "He's a nice guy. I think he's a little overwhelmed."

Renee chuckled. "It's no wonder. It's a whole other world for him, too."

"Jasmine has a crush on him," Tim said. "She keeps making Hunter sit somewhere else so Art can sit by her."

"That's so sweet," Renee said. "And so was you sending me flowers. Thank you so much."

"You're welcome."

Being with Tim was always so easy, just like it was that evening. There were never any awkward silences and they had plenty to laugh about. He never failed to ask about her day and he was genuinely interested.

As they finished dessert, Renee asked, "Would you like to see my humble abode?"

"I'd love to."

—∾—

Renee let them in. "I didn't think about it being dark in here. Well, at least it's empty so there's nothing to trip over. It won't be a long tour since there're only the three rooms and a tiny water closet."

"There's enough moonlight," he said. "The kitchen is a decent size."

"Yes. I was surprised. I was expecting it to barely have enough room to turn around in," she said. "And there's a pantry, too. I know that's probably not very important to you, but it is to me."

He smiled. "It would be if I was moving into my own place. You have to have somewhere to put food."

"You'd have to know how to cook first," she said.

"I know how to cook. I asked Cora to show me some things."

"Really? I didn't know that."

Tim said, "I'll cook for you sometime."

"I accept," Renee said.

They finished looking around.

"It's a nice apartment, Renee. I'll be happy help you paint," he said.

"You're full of surprises. I didn't know you know how to paint, either," she said.

"Yep. Construction, painting, wallpapering, all kinds of stuff like that," Tim said. He held out a hand to her. "May I have the honor of having the first dance in your new home with you?"

"I'd be delighted," Renee said, moving into his arms.

It didn't matter that there was no music as they waltzed around the small parlor. They could imagine the music in their heads and she followed his lead. Watching Renee's beautiful face in the moonlight, Tim thought he'd never get tired of looking at her. She was graceful and her lush body in his arms tantalized his senses.

After what seemed an appropriate length of time for a song, Tim halted. "Thanks for the dance, honey."

"Thank you," she said.

Their eyes met and held. Tim tipped her chin up a little, dipping his head to brush his lips against hers. She didn't pull away from him, so he did it again, only a little firmer this time. Her lips were even softer than they looked and tasted of the wine they'd drunk at dinner. He put his arms around her waist, pulling her closer.

No one had ever kissed Renee like Tim did, so softly, and it was incredibly seductive. He coaxed and asked instead of demanding. She put her arms around his neck and he tightened his hold on her a little. Still, he silently asked and she answered in the affirmative by becoming slightly more aggressive.

Tim let her set the pace, willing to follow where she led. Even as the kiss deepened, he took his time, enjoying every second of what he hoped would be the first of many kisses they would share. It was clear that Renee was a very experienced kisser, which didn't bother Tim at all—except that he wanted to be the only man she kissed from now on.

Slowly, he brought the kiss to an end and then just stood still.

"Renee, can I tell you something?" His voice had grown deeper with passion.

"Of course," she whispered, shaken.

"That has to be the best first kiss I've ever had," he said, opening his eyes.

The smoky look in them set her pulse skipping along and she said, "Me, too. I wasn't expecting that. I didn't know what to expect, really, but not that. I mean, I expected it to be good, but that was amazing, yes, amazing is a good word, or maybe powerful—I sound like Pa!"

They laughed and Tim said, "Speaking of which."

She giggled while he grinned.

"This isn't meant to pressure you in any way, but I had a very nice conversation with your pa today and he said it would be all right if I dated you. Like I said, I'm not forcing myself on you, I'm just letting you know that if you wanted to, there wouldn't be an issue with your parents," Tim said.

Renee couldn't believe it at first, but then she remembered his comments about a man not letting anything stop him from seeing a woman if he was really interested in her. He'd meant what he said, and he'd backed it up, too.

"You asked Pa for his permission to court me?"

"That's right."

She held his gaze. "Why would you do that?"

"Because you haven't been out of my mind ever since we danced at Devon's wedding."

Renee shook her head a little. "Why didn't you say anything?"

"I'm not sure, really. I think I wanted to get to know you better before I actually asked you out. I guess I didn't want there to be any pressure; you probably get that enough. I wanted to be different than the other guys you've been out with," he said.

Tim was showing Renee that there was a whole other side to him besides the good-time cowboy. "You certainly are different, and I mean that in a good way. You're always doing little things for me and you're very gentlemanly. And so much fun. Of course all you Dwyers are, so I'm not surprised about that."

"Yeah, you've had enough adventures with Jr. and Skip," Tim said.

"I still can't believe that Joey's married," she said.

"Me, neither." He slid his arms around her waist again. "So what do you think? Would you like to be my little snuggle bunny?"

"Snuggle bunny?" she asked, giggling.

Tim grinned. "It's a little-known fact that snuggle bunny is an old Scottish term of endearment."

"Really?"

"Really. It's from around 1680 or so. Chester told me that a while back," he said.

"Snuggle bunny. I like that." Renee wasn't sure what to say. "Can I think about it?"

Tim was thrilled that she hadn't said no. He could be patient a while longer. "Of course. No pressure, remember?"

"I remember."

"Well, I better get you home. We both have work in the morning," he said. "How are those pillowcases coming along?"

"Good," she said, locking the door.

It didn't take long for him to drop Renee off and when he did, he only kissed her briefly, keeping things light and pressure-free. He surprised himself by the level of restraint he was able to maintain around her. Maybe it was just that he'd never cared about a woman so much. He watched until she was inside before driving away, smiling as he relived their kiss.

"He wants me to be his snuggle bunny."

Marcus looked up from the newspaper article he was reading to see Renee closing the door to his office. "Huh?"

Renee had always felt comfortable talking to Marcus about anything. He had a unique ability to put people to ease and he never gave the impression that he didn't care.

"Tim. He asked me last night if I wanted to be his snuggle bunny."

Marcus laughed. "I've never heard that expression. It's cute, though."

"He says it's an old Scottish pet name."

"Ah. I see," Marcus said. "And what did you say?"

"That I'd think about it."

Her coy expression amused him. "Playing hard to get, huh?"

"No, not exactly. I really did want to think about it a little. He's so different from other men. He listens to me and he cares about what I think."

Marcus leaned back in his chair, propping his right ankle up on his opposite knee. "That's a good thing. It shows that he really cares about you and that he's not just lookin' for a good time."

"What if I mess things up between us, Marcus?" Renee asked. "I'm scared that I'll lose him completely."

"Yeah, that's a tough decision. Trying to be both friends and lovers is hard unless your lover is also your best friend. Like me and Claire," he said. "You'll never know if you don't take a risk. Relationships can be risky, but in my opinion, you and Tim laid a little bit of a foundation, so it might not be as risky as two people who just start seeing each other romantically right away." He smiled. "Do you *want* to be his snuggle bunny?"

Renee giggled and blushed. "Listen to me—and I hardly ever blush!" She put her hands to her hot cheeks.

Marcus' warm laughter filled the office. "I'd say that's a yes. Whenever a girl giggles and blushes, it means yes."

"He sent me the most beautiful red roses yesterday and he took me to dinner, too."

"Boy oh boy! You better snap him up, girl. Rope him and hog tie him before some other filly gets to him," Marcus said. "That's what Seth would say."

She stomped her feet a little before getting up. "I think I will! Thanks, Marcus. I don't know what I'd do without you."

"Anytime," he said, smiling as she left. "Snuggle bunny," he mumbled and went back to reading his article.

On her lunch break, Renee popped in to see her mother. They'd been working out their differences since the night they'd fought.

"Hi, honey," Hope said.

"May I use your phone for three minutes? That's all the longer I'll be. I don't want to tie the line up in case there's an emergency," she said.

One of the things Hope loved about Renee was her sense of responsibility. "And I suppose you'd like me to step out for those three minutes?" she teased Renee.

"Please? I'll tell you all about it when I'm done. I just can't do it with you here beside me," Renee said.

Hope put her pen down. "I suppose. Actually, I don't mind. I need to go get some coffee anyway."

She left, closing the door after her, and Renee picked up the receiver.

"Switchboard," said Black Fox.

Renee smiled at his no-nonsense greeting. "*Han*, Grandfather."

"*Hau*, Granddaughter. I heard that you rented an apartment."

"Boy, word travels fast," Renee said.

"Yes. It is a small town."

"Very true. Would you put me through to the Dwyers, please?"

"Yes." He came back in a moment. "I have Chester for you. Go ahead."

"Oh, Grandfather, I'll be exactly two minutes." This indicated that she didn't want him to listen the way that operators sometimes had to so they knew when a call ended.

"Ok. Two minutes. Here is Chester."

"Thanks. Chester? It's Renee Keller."

"Hello, Miss Keller. How may I help you?"

"Would you be a dear and fetch Tim for me, but only if he's up at the house. I don't want to disturb him if he's in the middle of something. But don't tell him who it is," she said.

"Certainly. I believe he's in the playroom. One moment."

Tim came on the line in a few moments. "Hello? Who's this?"

"It's your snuggle bunny," she said, muffling a giggle.

He laughed. "It is, huh? You mean the snuggle bunny I kissed last night?"

"The very same."

"Mmm. I like the sound of that."

"I'm glad. Now, I only have a minute left before Grandfather comes back on the line. I'd still like to come over to see Kyle tonight. Is he going to be home?"

"Yeah. Come for supper."

"Ok. I'll see you then. Snuggle Bunny signing off."

He chuckled. "See you then."

Once they hung up, Tim let out a whoop and ran out of Joe's important office, almost colliding with his mother. He grabbed her and danced around with her in the hallway.

"What's going on?" she asked, laughing.

"I am officially courting Renee Keller. That's what's going on," he said.

Lacey's eyes widened. "You are? I thought you were just friends."

"Well, things sort of developed. I already asked Switch and he gave me his blessing," Tim said.

Lacey hugged him. "I'm so happy for you."

"Me, too. She's so beautiful, Mama. And funny and kind and sweet," Tim said. "Well, I better get back to it. I have to get that mare ready for Captain Davis to try out when he gets here. See ya later."

Chapter Eight

On Saturday, Tim, Switch, Skip, Devon, and Sawyer helped Renee paint her apartment. She'd elected to paint the kitchen a soft, buttery yellow, and the parlor, bedroom, and water closet a pretty cream. Renee had never painted before. Her attempts were clumsy and had to be gone over by someone else.

Switch finally sat her on a stepstool and said, "You sit here and look pretty and we'll finish this."

"Is that your way of saying I stink at this, Pa?"

"Yes," he said, laughing.

"You're awful. But you're right," she said. "I know. I'll go to the bakery and get us a treat."

"All right," Switch said, going back to his painting.

Tim watched her leave, his gaze roaming over her shapely, jeans-clad backside while Switch's back was towards him. He smiled and turned around to see Devon grinning at him.

"Shut up," he said.

They'd been out almost every night, including last night when they'd cleaned up pretty good at the Howler again. He'd tried to give her his half of their winnings, but she'd turned him down again. He liked that she didn't want money from him. Some women would since he was rich, but Renee wouldn't hear of it.

She returned with all sorts of pastries and some sandwiches. Once the painting was done, which didn't take long, they all sat down on the floor and ate the goodies. Switch watched the byplay between Tim and Renee and he was glad he'd given Tim permission to see his daughter. Tim was gentlemanly and respectful of Renee and Switch's confidence in their relationship grew.

A week later, Renee was set to spend her first night in her new apartment. D.J. and Frankie Samuels had come through with a nice bedroom suit and refused to take money from her. She decided that she was going to make them a nice quilt as repayment for the furniture. Switch and Hope had bought her a kitchen table and chairs. Her parlor now contained a matching blue and gold sofa and wingback chair, a coffee table, and two end tables.

Tim had bought her an Edison Pathe windup record player and several records, telling her that it was a late Valentine's Day present. Renee loved the ornate cabinet and she looked forward to hosting little dances for her family and friends. She and Tim had already tried the record player out and it had excellent sound quality.

That night, her family stayed for quite a while, loathe to leave her. Skip sulked a little. He and Renee were close and he was going to miss having her at home to talk to whenever he wanted. Finally, they left, and Renee changed into her nightclothes and fixed some tea. She liked working in her kitchen and was happy with how the apartment had turned out, thanks to all of her helpers.

She took the tea into the parlor and put a record on the player. Sitting down on the sofa, she put her feet up and picked up a magazine she'd bought that day. She'd begun reading an article on quilting when someone knocked on her door.

Going to it, she asked, "Who is it?"

"Hello, Snuggle Bunny."

She smiled as she opened the door. "Come on in, handsome."

He took in the sight of her in her pretty nightgown and practically salivated. Her lustrous dark hair flowed over her shoulders in waves and the garment left no doubt that she was a woman. "Good God, you look good enough to eat," he blurted.

Renee laughed. "Thank you. What's in the basket?"

Tim opened it and took out a fluffy orange kitten. "I thought you might get a little lonely, so I brought you a buddy to keep you company."

"He's so cute!" She cuddled the little feline, who purred when she scratched behind his little ears. "Thank you so much."

"You're welcome. His teeth are little, so I brought you some crushed-up chicken to get started with. I also put a couple of little tin dishes in here for food and water."

Her eyes held wonder. "You think of everything, don't you?"

He smiled. "I try. How's it going so far?"

"Fine. The family left not long ago. I was just having some tea and reading while I listened to music on the splendid phonograph a very handsome man gave me."

"Well, he must think an awful lot of you to do something like that," Tim said.

"Yes, he must. Thank you again."

"No need to thank me. Well, I'll let you get back to your reading. I just wanted to drop off your new roommate."

"Oh, no. I'm not letting you get away that fast," she said. "Would you like a drink? I have some scotch."

He smiled. "Who am I to turn down a nice offer like that?"

"Good. Here, you hold Romeo while I fix it. I had ice delivered today. Do you want some in your scotch?" she asked.

"No, thanks," he said sitting down on the sofa.

"Very well," she said, going into the kitchen.

She thought it was so nice fixing a drink for them in her new little place. She cut up some cheese, put a few pieces of chocolate bar on a plate, and set it all on a tray.

"What did you do?" he asked as she set the tray on the coffee table. "You didn't have to go to any trouble."

She sat down by him. "It's no trouble at all." She handed him his drink and took her own.

Tim raised his glass. "A toast to your new home. May you have good times and happiness here."

"Hear, hear," she said as they clinked glasses and each took a sip. She tucked her feet up under her. "So, tell me about your day."

As he did, he could hardly take his eyes off her. They ate their snack and talked about all sorts of things. She found that Tim was hands on, but in a nice way. He squeezed her hand here and there and wound a long tendril of her hair around his fingers. He'd never done that before and she surmised that he must have been holding back because their relationship hadn't been romantic at the time.

She liked his gentle touch and the way he looked her in the eye as they spoke. He wasn't constantly ogling her and he paid attention to what she said. The kitten had gotten brave and jumped off the couch to explore his new home. He got frisky and started playing with his tail. They laughed at his antics and Renee thanked Tim again for giving him to her.

"Well, I know you have to work tomorrow, so I'd better let you get some rest," he said.

"All right, although I'm not sure how much I'll sleep. I'm a little wound up about sleeping in a new place," she said, running a hand over his arm. "Will you stay just a little longer?"

Her touch set him on fire and he thought, *I'll do anything you want.* "Sure. What were you reading?"

She moved closer to him, her hand moving up to caress the nape of his neck. "Nothing that would interest you."

The look in her eyes fanned the flames of his desire and Tim put an arm around her. "Do you have any idea how beautiful you are?"

She gave him a seductive smile. "I might have been told that a few times."

"Well, you are, and I'm gonna go crazy if I don't kiss you right now," he said.

He was surprised when she rose up, pressing her mouth to his, and sliding her arms around his neck. He wasn't going to refuse the chance to hold her and kiss her. He pulled her against him, kissing her urgently.

Tim's kisses were unlike anything Renee had ever known before and she couldn't get enough. He knew what he was doing and he was thorough. He tasted of scotch and chocolate and it was a heady combination of flavors. His lips were warm and soft. She lightly bit his lower lip and he growled against her mouth, burying his hands in her hair.

His lips left hers to press kisses along her throat down to her collar bone. "You smell so good," he said, inhaling her slightly floral scent.

"Thank you," she said, threading her fingers through his short hair.

Tim shuddered slightly at her touch and knew he was reaching the point of no return. He was perfectly willing, but he didn't want to move too far too fast. Reluctantly, he pulled away from her. "I better go before something happens that we're not ready for."

Renee appreciated his consideration. "That's probably a good idea, but for the record, you're hard to resist."

"Likewise," he said.

He got up and she followed him to the door. "Goodnight, Timmy."

"Goodnight, Snuggle Bunny," he said, giving her a last kiss.

She locked the door after him and then sighed. "How am I supposed to sleep after that?"

She fed Romeo and then took him to bed with her. He curled up on her pillow with her, his presence comforting to her in the new place. Eventually, her eyes drifted shut and she slept soundly.

Art watched Hailey fire off four arrows at a target. They pierced the target, forming a small cluster in the center of it.

He let out a low whistle. "We shoulda let you fight with us. I see what Kyle meant now."

It still rankled with Hailey that Kyle had turned her in. "Yes, you should have, but that can't be changed now."

He heard the irritation in her voice. "I'm sorry, Hailey, but he did the right thing."

Her eyes flashed silver fire at him. "I don't want to talk about it. We'll only wind up arguing. Men will always think that women are inferior to them."

She walked to the target and angrily extracted the arrows from it. His eyes followed her, drinking in her beauty in the buckskin leggings, buckskin shirt, and high moccasin boots. Her hair was growing out, but it was still only a little bit below her ears.

"It ain't that you're inferior, it's that there's one area where you're vulnerable and there are men who wouldn't think twice about taking advantage of it," he said.

"That may be true for some women, but I'm not like them. Anyone who tries anything like that with me will wind up dead," she said. "I'm as good a warrior as any man."

He could see he wasn't going to change her mind about it. "You're right. We're gonna argue about this. Best to drop it."

She gave him a curt nod and went back to practicing, although it didn't look like she needed to practice to Art.

"Do you hunt?" she asked.

"It's been a while, but yeah."

Flicking a glance at him, she asked, "Would you like to go hunting with me tomorrow morning? We go every morning."

He jumped at the chance to spend more time with her. "Sure. What time?"

"Five-thirty. Don't be late," she said. "There is a meadow where I go."

"Ok. I'll be here."

"Do you like your new job?"

Joe had given Art a job over at the Benson ranch where he kept twenty-five of their horses since their property couldn't handle any more horses than they already had. Art did everything from grooming and exercising horses to repairing fences.

"Yeah. It's the best job I ever had, and Caleb is a fair man. Has a good sense of humor, too."

"The Bensons are good people."

"Yeah. There's one fella over there that don't care for me, but I can deal with him," Art said.

As they talked, Hailey cast furtive glances at Art. She judged him to be around six-foot-two and somewhere around the one hundred eighty mark. He was muscular and handsome. His mixed heritage was evident in his light brown skin that reminded her of nutmeg. Art was quick to smile and liked to tease people. His teeth were a beautiful shade of white and Hailey found herself wondering what it would be like to kiss his sensual mouth.

Hailey wasn't accustomed to having those sorts of thoughts and found it disconcerting. She'd only been kissed once and that hadn't gone well. The boy had gotten frustrated because she hadn't known what to do and he'd never kissed her again. *Would Art be different?* she wondered. She quickly shoved her musings aside. She could tell that he was attracted to her; there were times when she could feel his gaze on her and it was exciting and confusing at the same time.

"I'm sure you can," she said. "Don't worry about him."

"I ain't. Well, I better get back to work. I'll see you tomorrow morning," Art said.

Hailey said, "If you're not busy tonight, you could come play knuckles or chess. Uncle bought a board."

Her invitation surprised him. Could it be that she liked him? "I'd like that."

She gave him a rare smile and it transformed her face from beautiful to stunning. "Good. I look forward to beating you."

He chuckled. "We'll see about that. I'll be seein' you."

She smiled as he walked away and then sent more arrows into the target.

Chapter Nine

Hunting with Hailey was an education for Art and he was further impressed with her prowess with a bow and arrows. Both of them brought down a buck, although he used a rifle. Hailey didn't shy away from field dressing her buck and she carried it home on her own, too. He helped her butcher them and he said that they could have his deer since he had no need of it.

"Thanks for havin' me along today," he said. "I had a good time, and I had a good time last night, too."

"Me, too," she said, smiling shyly.

Art looked around to make sure that no one else was in hearing distance. "Hailey, do you have a fella?"

Her eyes widened a little. "No, I don't."

"In that case, would you have dinner with me?" he asked.

Hailey froze in place, suddenly frightened. She'd never had a man ask her out before. "You want to have dinner with me? Are you sure? I'm not like other women. I'm not soft and feminine the way men want their women to be."

The way his eyes traveled over her made her feel warmer. "I want you just like you are. I like your fierceness and sharp edges, although maybe they could be a little softer where I'm concerned?"

Her cheeks turned a little pink and she gave him a coy smile. "Maybe a little bit. I'll have dinner with you. Where? I need to know how to dress."

"How about we start with the Grady House? Not so fancy at first?"

"Ok."

"Is six ok?" he asked.

"Yes."

"See you then, my feisty bravette," he said. He'd picked up the expression from the Dwyers.

"Goodbye."

Hailey smiled to herself as she went back to work, anticipation building inside as she thought about the coming evening.

Art cleaned up after the long day of work, washing off the dust and sweat. He'd picked up a few new pairs of jeans and button-down shirts at Elliot's. He put on a pair of the jeans and a white shirt. Shrugging into a denim coat, he looked in the mirror and decided he looked presentable.

He saddled the horse he'd been given to use and headed for the Lakota camp. Like Kyle, he was adjusting to the complete change in his life from his time in the military. It still didn't seem real to be back in "regular" society and it certainly didn't seem real to be going out with a beautiful woman.

As he neared the camp, he let out a low whistle, knowing that ever since the Loyalty party had attempted to raid the camp last year, Black Fox had reinstated the practice of keeping sentries on guard. Art couldn't blame him.

He passed without being detained and rode over to Raven and Zoe's house, waving at people and saying hello. When he knocked on the door, Raven opened it and came outside, closing the door behind him. Art arched an eyebrow at his hard look.

"You are taking Hailey to dinner."

"Yes, sir," Art said, a slight feeling of trepidation rising.

Raven's eyes glittered with warning. "She has never been courted.

Hailey is courageous, tough, and hard sometimes, but inside beats the heart of a woman all the same. I warn you that if you hurt her, I will not hesitate to act. Have I made myself clear?"

"Yes, sir. I'll be good to her."

Raven gave him a measuring look and then smiled. "I believe you. Have a nice time."

"Thanks." He sighed in relief when Raven motioned for him to follow him inside. He greeted Zoe and exchanged pleasantries with her.

When Hailey came into the parlor, Art had to work hard not to gawk. After seeing her in only military and Red Cross uniforms and buckskin, the simple green wool skirt and white shirtwaist looked exotic on her.

Raven and Zoe hid smiles when they saw how shyly Hailey glanced at Art.

"Well, Miss Dwyer, you look pretty," he said.

Although Hailey's skin color was darker than Zoe's her blush was still visible and her parents again had to stifle smiles. They hadn't seen her blush since she'd been a teenager.

"Thank you," she said quietly.

"I miss the bow and arrows, though," he joked.

She smiled. "Do you want me to take them along?"

"Nah. Maybe next time," he said.

Hailey took her coat down from a peg by the front door and became confused when he held out his hand for it. She hesitantly gave it to him as though afraid he was going to steal it. It was a bizarre experience for her to have someone hold her coat for her. She'd seen men do it for other women, including Raven with Zoe, but no one had ever offered to perform the gentlemanly act for her before.

Once she had it on, they said goodbye to Raven and Zoe.

Hailey said, "We have a car around back. I can't ride a horse in this thing."

Art couldn't hold back a laugh. "Boy, you're really not used to dressing like that, are you?"

"No," she said. "I warned you."

"Yes, you did."

He insisted on cranking the Model T to life. Then he hopped in and they took off.

—ϖ—

Art had never been so entertained by a woman before. Hailey was a contradiction in every way. He'd almost had to argue with her in order for her to allow him to seat her. However, she ate almost daintily and was animated with her family, who greeted her and Art.

Hailey was grateful for the distraction because she had no idea what to say to Art. It had been easy being around him when they'd been overseas because they had the war to talk about and war-related subjects. Eventually though, they were left alone and she felt awkward again.

Her discomfort was almost palpable and Art hated seeing her so tense.

"How old were you when you started hunting?" he asked.

Her smile returned. "Father took me to snare rabbits when I was six. I caught on quickly. Then he made me my own little bow and arrows. I still have it. I kept all of the bows and arrows he made me as I grew. Grandfather made me a few, too. I love hunting, even when I don't catch anything. Being in nature is calming and there's much to learn there. Poor Ma. She missed out on having daughters as feminine as she is. Snow Song isn't as tough as I am, but she's not like Ma, either."

Art said, "I'm sure she's real proud of you for going overseas with the Red Cross. Do they know about you fighting for those two weeks?"

She laughed. "Yes. Ma was … horrified, but Father and Grandfather were proud and liked that I pulled one over on the army."

Art grinned and shook his head. "I'm sure they did. They have their own history with them."

"Not the modern army. They don't hold any of them responsible for the things that happened in the past. In fact, they urged our Lakota men to enlist and fight for our country. Times are changing and we're changing with them. There's not much of a choice," she said.

"No, I guess not," Art said. "They can't change fast enough for some things." He'd noticed the way a few people were looking at him and knew that in most places whites and black were segregated, with coloreds only allowed to eat in certain places.

Hailey, too, had noticed and she glared back defiantly at a few people until they dropped their eyes. "Pay them no mind. They know better than to bother me."

"I'm glad for that," Art said. "I'm not afraid of them, though. Don't worry about that. I've dealt with my fair share of that sort of thing."

"I'm sure you're fierce in battle. I would have liked to have seen you fight."

He smiled. "Don't start that again."

"I don't know what you're talking about," she said with a sly grin.

"Mmm hmm."

They finished their meal and Art grabbed the bill before Hailey could. He saw that he was going to have to educate her about some things relating to men and women. Hailey grew increasingly nervous on the way home. She pulled over near the entrance of the camp road and put the car in park.

"What's the matter?" Art asked.

"I don't know how to do this. I can't do this. I tried one time and it didn't end well."

"Hailey, don't fall apart on me. It was just dinner," Art said. "I ain't askin' you to marry me or anything."

"You mean a friendly dinner?"

Art chuckled. "How about a little bit more than a friendly dinner. Can you handle that?"

Some of Hailey's anxiety eased. "Yeah. I can do that."

"Ok. Good, because I'd like to do it again sometime."

"You would? Why? I'm a horrible date."

"Hailey, shut it down," Art said.

"Why?"

"Because I wanna talk about this. Shut it down."

Hailey cut the engine and waited expectantly as quiet settled around them.

"Now, why do you think you're a bad date?"

"I'm sure you'd rather be with a woman who's feminine and pretty and talks about womanly things. I'm not like that at all. I don't care about any of that."

"I don't care about that stuff, either. If I'd wanted to ask out someone like that, I wouldn't have asked you," Art said. "I understand that you're scared, but there isn't any reason to be. I don't wanna talk about dresses and whatever else some women talk about. I wanna talk about whatever comes to mind, and if we're quiet, that's fine, too. You're makin' this more complicated than it has to be."

"I don't know how to flirt and I don't know how to … kiss right," she said.

"Hmm. That's funny because I watched you flirt with a whole bunch of troops back in France and it sure felt like you knew how to kiss when you kissed me on New Year's Eve. And I wasn't the only one you kissed," Art said.

"That doesn't count. I was half-drunk that night," she said, grinning. "People can do things when they're drunk that they wouldn't do when they're sober."

"Ok, so I'll get you half-drunk and then kiss you."

Hailey laughed. "You might have to. Besides, that was just a friendly kiss."

"I'll settle for a friendly kiss here and there," Art said.

"I flirted?"

Art couldn't believe that she didn't know she'd been flirting left and right in France. "You have no idea, do you?" he said, laughing. "No clue why the card games you were involved in were the most popular. You had those boys eating out of the palm of your hand. The way you teased them and made them laugh."

Hailey's forehead creased. "I did? I was just treating them like I do my brother and cousins. I act the same way with them, too."

"Well, that may be, but those men ate it up. You were easy to be around and you didn't care what you said, which was refreshing. No one has to guess where they stand with you and sometimes that's nice. A lot of women are hard to read. You're not, and I like that."

"You do?"

"Yeah. Boy, you made a lot of those nurses and other women jealous."

"Me? Why?"

Art passed a hand over his face. "Because of what I just told you. Think of how many guys wanted to dance with you and they all wanted to talk to you. You're different. You're the girl who wears her hair short and looks better than half the women there with it that way."

Looking back, Hailey saw that it was true. She'd been popular, but she didn't know it was because the men had found her beautiful. She'd thought it was because they thought of her as one of the guys, a tomboy.

"You didn't see any of those guys kissin' other guys on New Year's Eve, did you?"

"No."

"No, but they wanted to kiss you the same way I did. I'm just lucky enough that you and Dwyer are cousins and I got to come home with him and see you," Art said. "Some of the other women gave out kisses, but some wouldn't. But you were fearless about it. That's another reason I like you."

"I don't think I'm beautiful," she said, running a hand over her short hair.

"Well, you are."

"Hmm. You should have kept me in the battle with you. We could have found a trench for two," Hailey said, batting her eyelashes at him.

Art broke into laughter. "Damn! You're right! I shoulda. I'd have kicked Dwyer out, too."

"Told you," she said.

"See? That's what I mean. Don't tell me you don't know how to flirt." He was glad to see her confidence returning.

"Thanks, Art."

"For what?"

"Making this easier and for making me feel better about myself," she said, meeting his eyes.

"My pleasure. I'll start her up," he said, getting out.

In a few short minutes, they arrived in camp and parked behind her house. When they got out, Art took her hand and it felt natural to Hailey. His hand was strong and it felt nice wrapped around hers.

Art chuckled.

"What?" Hailey asked.

"I was just remembering that handshake you gave me when you jumped down in our trench. I had no clue you were a woman. I thought you were just a young kid. It's no wonder you fooled everyone," he said. "But I like holding your hand this way better."

"Me, too," Hailey said.

He shook her hand a little. "So are you gonna teach me how to snare rabbits tomorrow morning?"

"If you want me to."

"I want you to. Same time as today?"

"Yeah."

He raised her hand, giving the back of it a quick kiss. "Goodnight, soldier," he said, mounting his horse.

"Goodnight."

She watched Art ride across the clearing to the trail that would take him to the Benson ranch.

Art hadn't gotten too far before he heard someone call his name. He stopped his horse and turned around. Hailey jogged in his direction.

"What are you doing?" he asked.

Hailey gathered her courage. "I didn't get my friendly kiss goodnight."

"I didn't get mine, either."

"I think we should fix that, Corporal Perrone."

"I think you're right," he said, dismounting.

Hailey didn't allow herself to think about what she was doing. She just put her arms around Art's neck and pressed her lips to his. When he cupped the back of her head lightly and held her in place, she stiffened a little and then relaxed when he softly stroked her cheek with his thumb.

Art ended the kiss in increments and looked into her eyes. "That was some friendly kiss, Dwyer."

"I'll say."

He smiled and stepped back from her. "You better get back before your pa thinks I kidnapped you."

Hailey arched an eyebrow. "I don't need permission to go anywhere or do anything."

"Yeah, yeah."

As he rode away, Art was glad that she couldn't see the broad grin on his face, but if he'd have been looking back at her, he would have seen the same grin on hers.

Chapter Ten

Renee smiled to herself as she closed her apartment door after kissing Tim goodnight. She locked it and picked up Romeo when he came to her. It was now almost the end of April and the past month had been magical. Tim was everything a woman dreamed about. She kept scolding him about it, but he spoiled her terribly and he wouldn't stop. They had so much fun together and he made her feel cherished.

She pet and played with Romeo as she changed for the night. Then she went to the kitchen to fix some tea. The cook stove was only lukewarm, so she stirred up the coals and put on some small pieces of wood that would catch fire quickly. Tim always made sure to bring an armload of wood up with him whenever he came. He did little things like that for her all the time.

Someone knocked on her door and she chuckled. Tim sometimes came back like that for one more kiss goodnight or just to tell her something he'd forgotten.

She opened the door. "What is it this ti—"

Her smile died when she found herself facing two men with what looked like pillowcases over their heads. She tried to close the door on them, but the first one caught the door and shoved it open, knocking her backwards forcefully. Renee tripped over the shoes she'd kicked off when she'd arrived home. She stumbled and went down. Immediately, she tried to scramble to her feet, but her nightgown hampered her movements.

A hard kick to her ribs flipped her over and she screamed. It was cut short when one of the attackers cracked her across the face. Then the man roughly grabbed her face, squeezing it hard.

"Ready for some fun, sweetheart?" he asked.

"No. No. Please don't," she said. "Please leave."

"Well, you have good manners, but we're not going anywhere just yet."

Her face and ribs ached, but Renee's strong spirit rose and she decided that this wasn't going to happen without a fight.

"I asked nicely," she said before boxing him hard on both ears at the same time.

She hadn't spent so much time around the Lakota without learning a few things. Although she wasn't a proficient fighter, she was strong from the sort of work she did, and her anger gave her added strength. The man cried out in pain and Renee struggled out of his grasp. If she could just get to the kitchen and grab a knife she might have a chance.

She made it to her feet before the other man tackled her, bringing her back down to the floor with him. He flipped her over and hit her several more times until she almost lost consciousness. Renee lost track of time after that and wished more than anything that she had passed out. Finally her torment ended and blackness eventually claimed her.

Tim whistled as he jogged up the stairs to Renee's apartment the next morning. He was going to surprise her by cooking her breakfast before she went to work and he carried a grocery bag with him. Reaching her door, he rapped on it.

"Good morning, Snuggle Bunny. Your chef has arrived," he called through the door. When she didn't come to the door, he knocked again.

He heard Romeo let out a squall and smiled. "Go get your mama, Romeo. Did she oversleep?" He knocked louder, but there was still no answer. "Renee!" She was always still home at that hour, so he thought it was odd that she didn't answer.

He tried the knob and found the door unlocked, which was also strange. She always kept the door locked. Opening the door slightly, Tim called out again, but still no answer. Then he saw her foot peeking around the doorway into the kitchen and the hair on the back of his neck rose in alarm.

"Renee?" He hurried to the kitchen and almost went down when he slipped on blood. *Renee's blood.* "Oh, God," he said, as he looked at her.

Her nightgown was torn and bloody and it seemed as though she was battered everywhere. He thought for sure that she was dead, but as he knelt next to her, he heard her take a breath.

"It's ok, honey. I'm gonna get you help. I'll be right back," he said before rushing downstairs. Sawyer wasn't at his shop yet, so Tim ran out into the street, ramming right into Lyla Samuels. He grabbed her by the shoulders. "Lyla, go to the telegraph office and call the hospital. Renee's been attacked. Have the doctors come and then call Mitch. Go! Hurry!"

Lyla didn't question him, taking off down the street as Tim ran back upstairs. He knelt next to Renee. He didn't know where to touch her, so he stroked her hair.

"I'm here. It's Tim. Help is coming. Hold on, Renee."

He ran into the parlor, snatching a quilt from the sofa and covering her with it. God only knew how long she'd lain there and it was chilly in the apartment now. Not caring if he got blood on himself, Tim lay down beside her, putting the quilt over the both of them to trap his body heat so that she would warm up that much quicker.

The whole time he waited for help to come, Tim talked to her, urging her to stay with him and telling her that it would be all right. It felt like forever, but it was only a matter of perhaps ten minutes before he heard multiple people on the stairs.

"Careful!" he shouted. "There's blood there. Don't slip on it."

Sheriff Mitch Taylor's face came into view as Tim looked at the kitchen doorway.

"I'm keepin' her warm. She's been attacked and she's hurt really bad. I don't know how long she's been here," Tim said.

"Ok, son," Mitch said calmly. *Good God,* he thought, looking at Renee. A couple of doctors are on their way. It's good that you're keeping her warm."

"I came to make her breakfast like I sometimes do and she didn't answer the door. She always answers. When she didn't, I tried the door and came in. That's when I saw her. I went to get help right away and sent Lyla."

"Ok, Tim," Mitch said as more people arrived. He moved back as Marcus came to the kitchen. "He's been keeping her warm. I don't know what you're going to find."

Marcus nodded curtly as he took in the scene before him. He saw the blood on the floor and the condition of Renee's face and clenched his teeth. "Tim, you did real good, but I need to get in there to assess her, ok?"

Tim nodded and pulled the quilt off her. Marcus barely suppressed a gasp. He traded spots with Tim and knelt beside her, listening to her heart and lungs to determine if there was any fluid buildup. Her heartbeat was a little sluggish, but not as much as he'd feared and her lungs were clear.

Marcus gently went over her, checking for broken bones that would need to be stabilized before they moved her. Finding none, he motioned for his nephew and fellow doctor, Mike Samuels, to come in with a stretcher. Carefully, they put her on it and covered her with several blankets. The doctors' eyes met, the same anger reflected in each gaze.

Slowly, they carried her downstairs, putting her in Flynn Booker's hearse. Dawson didn't have a dedicated ambulance at the time, so the hearse doubled as an ambulance, as was done by many communities at the time. Marcus climbed in with her and Flynn slowly pulled out onto the road.

Tim had ridden one of their horses into town and he mounted up, urging the stallion after the hearse.

By this time, the rest of the Kellers had been alerted and they were waiting when Renee was brought in. It took several people to keep them back so they could get Renee to the accident room.

Marcus stayed behind a moment to talk to the family.

"I know you're worried sick right now, but you have to let us do our jobs, folks," he said kindly. "We're gonna take good care of her and either Mike or myself will come out just as soon as we can."

Hope felt faint when she saw the blood on Marcus' white doctor's coat. He'd run out of the hospital without his overcoat. Switch put an arm around her when he saw her turn white.

"It's ok, honey," he said. "Marcus and Mike will help her."

Marcus kissed Hope's forehead and patted Switch's shoulder. "That's right. Just hang in there. You, too, Skip."

Skip nodded, tears sliding down his face. Switch guided Hope to a row of wooden chairs and sat down with her.

"Justin, come here," he said, patting the chair on the other side of him. When Skip sat down, Switch put his other arm around his son. "Now listen, you two. Renee is a strong girl and she's gonna make it through this. We have to be strong, too, so we can help her. She's in the best of care right now. Ok?"

Both of them nodded and gained strength from him. For his family's sake, Switch combatted the panic that gnawed at him. They needed him and he wasn't going to let them down by going off the deep end.

Tim came running into the lobby, saw them, and changed direction. "Any news yet? No, of course not. They just got here. Sorry," he said, sitting down.

"What happened, Tim?" Switch asked, eyeing his bloody sack coat and shirt.

Tim told them but left out the more disturbing details, figuring that it wouldn't do them any good. Looking down at himself, he realized why Hope couldn't look at him.

"Oh, God."

He went over to the desk and asked Polly if he could use the telephone to call home. He asked Lacey to bring him a change of clothes. In the meantime, Polly gave him a clean sleeping shirt normally given to patients. Tim stepped into the washroom and changed into the sleeping shirt. Wadding up his clothes, he came out and asked Polly to throw them away. He never wanted to see them again.

Lacey and Joe showed up and Tim changed into the clothes she brought him. Lacey sat on the other side of Hope, offering her support and holding her hand. There wasn't much for them to do but wait. Tim sat silently, staring off into space, trying not to see Renee's battered form in his mind, but it was impossible.

He didn't realize that he was crying until he felt a hand on his arm and looked over to see his father sit down beside him. Joe put an arm around him and hugged him. Tim stayed there for a moment before his stomach rebelled and he ran outside, getting sick on the little lawn. Joe had followed him.

"Oh, Daddy, it was so horrible! And there wasn't much I could do. I tried to keep her warm, but I couldn't touch her. I didn't know where to because I didn't want to hurt her," Tim said. "She has to be ok, Daddy. She just has to be. I love her and I can't lose her."

Joe succeeded in stopping Tim's pacing and hugged him. "It's ok, son. She's gonna be all right. She's feisty and strong and she's got a lot of people praying for her. She'll pull through. Those doctors in there working on her are some of the finest doctors in the country as far as I'm concerned and they'll do everything in their power to make sure she's all right."

Tim took a shuddering breath and nodded against Joe's shoulder before pulling away. He wiped his tears away and composed himself. "I'm all right, Daddy," he said as Sawyer rode up on his horse.

Sawyer jumped down and came over to them. "How is she?"

"We don't know yet," Tim said.

"She's gonna make it, Tim. Renee's as tough as they come," Sawyer said. "If she can help break the mayor out of jail, she can pull through this. I came to help keep Skip calm."

"What do you mean?" Tim asked.

"Skip's not like Switch. It's never good if he stews too long. I'm afraid of him trying to find out who did this and going after them. He and Renee are really close and it's been hard on Skip not having her around at home much. He was the same way for a while after Jethro left home. I don't want Skip to get hurt, but I also don't want him to go to jail for murder. He's wicked with weapons when he chooses to be," Sawyer said. "Hang in there, Tim."

Tim nodded as Sawyer entered the hospital.

Joe gripped Tim's arms. "Listen to me, Tim. Under no circumstances do you turn vigilante. Renee needs you, and you can't help her if you're in jail. I know how you feel because of what happened to Emily. Had Abe lived, I would've been hard pressed not to go after him and put a bullet in his brain. Let Mitch and the boys do their jobs and don't interfere. Your place is here right now. Understand?"

Tim nodded. "Yeah, Daddy. You're right."

"Promise me, Tim."

"I promise."

"Good. Now let's go see if there's any news."

Chapter Eleven

Hope sat by Renee's bed, watching her sleep. She'd barely left her the past three days. Marcus was keeping Renee partially sedated to allow her to sleep through the worst of the pain.

I'm so sorry to have to tell you this, but Renee was sexually assaulted, and I'd say by more than one attacker. She's badly bruised in many places, but the only broken bone she has is just a small fracture to left forearm. There's no internal thoracic bleeding, but she's had other damage done internally. I know this may be embarrassing and disturbing, but you need to know everything so that you can help her.

When I performed Renee's internal examination, it showed that she's never been with a man before. The reason I mention this is because this will impact her mental state even more than it does a victim who wasn't a virgin. When the time is right, and that'll be up to her, Mike will help her and I'm sure that she's going to lean on you and her girlfriends. Mike and Hannah are the only other staff who know the full extent of Renee's condition and they'll keep it completely confidential ...

Those words, as kindly as Marcus had said them to her and Switch, would be forever etched into Hope's memory. Not only had Renee been brutally assaulted, but something very precious had been taken from her. Marcus was confident that all of Renee's physical injuries would heal, but the mental wounds would never completely go away. Religious beliefs aside, Hope knew that it was a woman's prerogative to whom she gave her virginity, and to have that choice taken away was doubly traumatic.

Fortunately, Hope had been able to choose Switch and he'd been gentle, kind, and funny on their wedding night. She'd wanted that same kind of experience for Renee; now she'd never know what it was like to give herself to someone for the first time. Was her internal damage so severe that she wouldn't be able to have children?

Hope agonized over her daughter and she wished that she could hold Renee and soothe away her pain.

Renee stirred and opened her one good eye, focusing on Hope. "Ma?" she whispered.

"I'm right here, sweetie," Hope said. "I'm right here." She kissed Renee's hand. "Are you thirsty?"

"Yes."

Hope helped Renee drink some water.

"Thank you. Is Pa here?" Renee's voice was slightly stronger. "Am I in the hospital?"

"Yes, honey. You're going to be all right. Pa will be back in just a little bit."

Renee nodded as her head rested on the pillow. "You're damn right I will be. Where's Skippy? I want to see Skippy."

Hope didn't think it was a good idea to let Skip see her at the moment as he had flown into a rage the first time he had seen her.

"Skip has football practice," Hope said, trying to put Renee off.

"Ok. I want to see him, Ma. I need to see him. And I want to talk to Sheriff Taylor, too."

"Renee, honey, you're not well enough yet," Hope said.

Renee gripped Hope's hand with surprising strength. "You have him come see me. I need to tell him what I remember. I want those bastards caught and I'm going to help put them behind bars. Get him, Ma. Please?"

Hope was amazed that Renee was thinking so clearly. She was also amazed that she was out for revenge instead of feeling afraid.

"Please, Ma."

It was Renee's prerogative to talk to Mitch and Hope didn't want to waste Renee's energy by arguing with her. "I don't want to leave you," she said.

Renee gave her a slight smile. "I'll be all right for just that little bit. Please call him." Switch appeared in the doorway. "Pa's here. He'll take good care of me."

"I sure will," Switch said.

Hope kissed her hand again. "All right."

She left as Switch sat down by her. "What can I get you, honey?" he asked.

"Skippy. I need to make sure he's all right," Renee said.

Switch's eyebrows drew together. "Renee, that's not a good idea right now. He's not doing well with this. Besides, you need to worry about yourself and rest right now."

She squeezed his hand. "Pa, you don't understand. What I need is to make sure he's all right so I don't have to worry about him. He'll be ok if I talk to him. And I need to help catch these animals."

Switch was further perplexed. "Aren't you scared?"

"To death, Pa, but I refuse to give in to that right now. Please get Skip for me," she pleaded with him. "And Tim, if he wants to see me. How horrible I must look, judging by how I feel. I don't even want to think about looking in a mirror."

Switch smiled. "Tim's been here to see you every day, so you don't have to worry about that."

"He has? I don't remember very much. Not until now," she said.

"I'll make a deal with you. I'll bring Justin if you rest until I do," Switch said.

"Deal."

"All right. When Hope gets back I'll go to the school and get him," he said, still apprehensive.

"Thank you," Renee said as her eyelids drifted shut.

Mason Taylor, lawyer and Dawson's football coach, watched Skip jump into the air to catch the ball that Tristan Cooper, their quarterback, had thrown. Skip's hands closed firmly around the ball and he brought it down with him. Instead of avoiding the defensive back standing in his way and streaking away like he normally did, the receiver rammed his shoulder into the other player.

Dirk Bradbury was caught off guard and went over backwards onto his rear end as Skip plowed him over and raced for the end zone. He outran a cornerback and made it across the line untouched.

"Whooo!" Skip said, spiking the ball.

Dirk was slow getting up.

"Keller! Come here!" Mason hollered from the sideline. "Get over here!"

Skip ran over to him, breathing hard. "Yeah, Coach?"

"Look, I know you're goin' through a rough time, but can you take it a little easy on our guys? We don't need anyone injured before the game on Friday."

"It's not my fault that Dirk wasn't ready. That's his job and mine is to get to the end zone. That's what I did," Skip said.

Mason's blue eyes narrowed. "Don't smart off to me, Skip. You get your head on straight or I'll bench you. Do you understand?"

Skip nodded. "Yeah. Sorry, Coach."

"It's ok." Mason shouted, "Ok, fellas! That's enough for today! Good work. See you tomorrow!"

As the boys headed for the school to change out of their uniforms, Skip heard, "Justin!" Recognizing his father's voice, he turned around and ran over to him.

"Hi, Pa."

"Hi. After you get changed, we're gonna go see Renee. She's asking for you, but you have to listen to me a minute. You can't fly off the handle like last time. I know you're angry and so are the rest of us, but you have to be calmer for her sake." Switch put a hand on his shoulder. "Can you do that?"

Skip smiled at the thought of seeing his sister. "Yeah. I'll behave. How is she?"

"It's the dangdest thing. She's mad and made Hope call Mitch to come see her. She wants to tell him what she remembers. She says she's scared, but she's angry more than anything right now," Switch replied as they walked towards the school.

"Good for her," Skip said emphatically. "I'll be right out."

Switch nodded. "I'll go get Dash for you."

"Thanks, Pa."

Tim quietly entered Renee's room, carrying a vase full of red roses, which he put on a stand by the windows. It tore at him every time he looked at her swollen, bruised face and he wanted to beat the scum who'd done this to her into a pulp. Swallowing down his rage, he approached her bed and sat down in the chair next to the right side of it.

He didn't want to wake her, but he wanted to hold her good hand. It bore traces of how hard she'd fought and tears formed in his eyes as he thought of how scared she must have been. He couldn't imagine what she'd endured and it made him sick to think about it. The need to touch her was too great to resist and he gently picked up her hand, holding it in both of his.

Renee felt his touch and smiled, opening her eyes. "Hi, Timmy," she said.

"Hi, honey," he said, wiping away a tear. "How are you feeling? Can I get you anything?"

She reached up to caress his cheek even though her muscles protested the motion. "Don't cry, Tim. Please don't."

More tears fell from his eyes even though he tried to check them. "I can't help it. I feel so bad about what happened. If only I'd stayed longer, maybe—"

"Shh. Don't you dare blame yourself. It's not your fault."

Tim dried his tears on his shirtsleeve. "Ok. I've been taking good care of Romeo for you."

She smiled. "Thank you."

"Listen, I was going to tell you over a nice dinner that I was gonna cook for you, but I want you to know that I love you, so much, Renee. I'm going to help you get through this. I'll be with you every step of the way and I'll do whatever you need me to. You're not alone and I'm not goin' anywhere," Tim said. "I love you and thought it was time you knew it."

More than anything in the world, his declaration of love comforted her and lifted her spirits. She tightened her hand around his. Ignoring the discomfort it caused, she gave him a big smile. "I love you, too, Timmy, and I can't tell you how relieved I am that you still want me. I've been worried about that today, but Pa said you've been here every day. I love you and I'm not letting you get away."

Leaning down, Tim gave her the gentlest of kisses as joy swept through him to know that she returned his feelings. "I love you so much. You make me so happy," Tim said.

"You make me happy," Renee said. "How could I not love you? You're handsome and kind and you make me laugh. And you cook. That's a big plus."

"And when you get out of here, I'll make you a nice dinner. How does that sound?" he asked.

"Wonderful. I'm actually hungry for the first time today," she said.

Tim kissed her hand and rose. "I know exactly what to get you. I'll be back in just a bit."

He left before she could object. She caught sight of the roses and smiled, knowing he'd brought them for her.

"Hey, sis," Skip said from the doorway.

"Skippy." She reached her hand out to him and he came over to take the chair Tim had vacated.

He took her hand. "It's good to see you awake."

"It's good to be awake," she said.

Shyly, Skip asked, "Are you in a lot of pain?"

"Yes, but they're giving me medicine. I'm going to be all right, but I need the help of my little brother," she said.

"How about your big brother?"

Renee gasped. "Jethro! What are you doing here?"

Jethro walked into the room, smiling at his siblings even as rage surged through him over Renee's appearance. While Renee and Skip resembled their father, Jethro looked like Hope with his blue eyes and golden hair. He was tall like Switch, however.

"I couldn't stay away when Pa told me what happened. He sent a telegram saying that you'd been hurt and I just had to come. So I got on a train immediately and got here as soon as I could," he said, sitting on the other side of her.

He went to hold her left hand but saw the cast on her forearm and just pat her upper arm instead.

"You shouldn't have interrupted your play to come here," Renee said.

Jethro shrugged. "That's what understudies are for. You're more important than any play, sis. How are you?"

"I'm better now that I have my brothers with me. Skip, you have to let go of your anger, ok? Please don't cause any trouble. For me?" she asked.

"Ok. I won't cause trouble," Skip agreed.

"Thank you."

Tim returned. "Oh, good Lord. Look what the cat dragged in," he said, smiling at Jethro.

Jethro laughed. "That's right. You better be treating my sister right, Dwyer."

Renee said, "He is. Don't worry about that," as the two men shook hands.

Tim said, "I brought you a strawberry milkshake and Reuben sandwich. Your favorite."

"That sounds delicious. I need to sit up more," she said.

Between the three men, they were able to get her propped up comfortably in the bed. It hurt to chew, but the sandwich was so tasty that she was willing to deal with it. The strawberry milkshake tasted heavenly and she was grateful to Tim for bringing her the food.

"That was just what I needed," she said. "How do you do that?"

Tim grinned unabashedly. “I’m good at being one step ahead of people. Plus, I pay attention.”

“Yes, you do,” Renee said.

Marcus stepped into the room. “Can anyone join the party?”

“Dr. Samuels, it’s so good to see you,” Jethro said.

Marcus forewent a handshake, hugging Jethro instead. “It’s good to see you, too, Jethro. You’re looking well.”

“Thanks. You’re not looking to shabby yourself.”

Marcus said, “Well, I’m trying to not look too old.”

Renee said, “You’ll always be a handsome man, Marcus.”

“Thanks. I hate to interrupt, but I’d like to check on my patient, gentlemen,” he said.

The three men stepped outside the room and Marcus closed the door.

Chapter Twelve

"You are not going back to your apartment and that's final," Switch said to Renee a week later.

Marcus pronounced her well enough to leave the hospital and she insisted on returning to her own place.

"Pa, I'll be all right," she said. "I don't want what happened to taint the happiness I've had there."

Switch was adamant. "I don't care about that. What I care about is you being safe, so you're coming home. It's the best thing for you so that we can take care of you. You're still weak and in pain. I'm done arguing about this. I'm putting my foot down."

Renee knew from the stubborn set of his jaw that it was futile to fight him further on it. He wasn't going to let her go back to her place and there was no way she could physically defy him about it.

"All right, Pa, but I'll go back there at some point."

His face tightened for a moment and then relaxed as he got a hold on his temper. "We'll see." The idea of her going back to that apartment at all repulsed him and he didn't want her staying there alone.

Hope arrived with her clothes and Switch left so Hope could help her change.

—ɱ—

Later that day, Renee was grateful to have come home. Leaving the safety of the hospital had been traumatic and she'd been grateful that she'd had so many people around her. Jethro and Skip had ridden in the back seat of their car with her, each of them putting an arm around her. She'd held their other hands tightly as she'd looked out the windows.

Now, as she sat on the sofa in their parlor, Renee was able to doze off and on. A knock came on their door and Hope opened it.

"Oh, hi, Tim," she said. "Come in." She eyed the basket he carried.

"Thanks. How's she doing?"

"Leaving the hospital was a little scary for her, but she's better now."

"I'm glad to hear that. I don't know how you feel about this, but I brought Romeo. He really misses her and I know she misses him. I thought it might help her to have him around," Tim said.

Hope smiled. "I think that's a good idea. I know she loves him. She's in the parlor."

"Thanks." Going into the parlor, he saw her on the sofa and stopped a moment. Her bruises were fading and much of the swelling was gone now. It was a relief to him to see her healing. "There's my Snuggle Bunny," he said.

Renee brightened immediately. "There's my handsome cowboy."

"I brought someone to see you." He opened the basket and lifted Romeo out.

"Oh! Look how big he got." Tim put Romeo on her lap and she pet him. He meowed and walked up to rub his face against her chin. Renee cuddled him and he purred happily.

"Sounds like he's happy," Tim said.

"Me, too," she said.

Tim sat down on the floor by the couch and they talked for about a half hour about normal, everyday subjects. Renee had told him this helped her focus on something else other than her traumatic experience. When he was ready to leave, he kissed her goodbye and stopped in the kitchen to say goodbye to Hope, who was fixing supper.

She surprised him by embracing him. "Thank you."

He returned her hug. "What for?"

"For standing by her and supporting her the way you have," Hope said. "Some men wouldn't."

Tim said, "I love her and that's what you're supposed to do for the people you love. I have some work to do tonight, but I'll come over in the morning, if that's all right?"

"Of course it is. You're welcome anytime, Tim," Hope said.

"Thanks. I'll see you all then."

When he left, Hope checked on Renee, who had fallen asleep with Romeo on her lap.

That afternoon, Randall told Joe that Jake had come to see him and Joe could immediately tell that something was very wrong.

"What happened?" Joe asked without preamble.

"They shut us down, Joe. They closed the Watering Hole. We're done, Joe." Jake's face was pink and sweat stood out on his forehead from stress. "What are we gonna do? I don't know how to do anything else but run a bar. It's been my life's work."

Joe sat down and ran a hand through his hair. "We knew it was comin' after they passed the state law last year banning alcohol. We've been lucky. I thought that we might be all right until it gets passed nationally, but I guess not. Don't panic, Jake. Sit down. It was the same with the gambling. A lot of the smaller towns like us were getting away with the gambling, but they'll be checkin' on a regular basis now."

Jake nodded. "Yeah. That puts an end to that, too. The police who came said that the Howler got shut down today too, so it's not just us. I guess that's a little consolation. They confiscated all of our inventory except for my private stash. We lost a lot of money."

Joe felt terrible about the closing of their beloved saloon, but more so for Jake than himself. The horse ranch was the Dwyers' main source of income, but for Jake, the Watering Hole was the only way he made a living. He'd done some investing at Joe's urging the past several years, but it wouldn't be enough to live on for very long.

It was a good thing that two of the Hendersons' three kids were employed outside of the saloon, but their son, Andy, worked alongside Jake running the bar. The Henderson men weren't the only ones the closure affected, though. Four bouncers were now out of work, although Rick Westlake had plenty of money to fall back on.

However, for Jamie Samuels and Zoe Dwyer, playing in the band was their only job. Luke, J.R., and Nate only worked to make a little extra money and have some fun, but they all had full-time jobs. In Seth's case, he was semi-retired from the ranch because of his leg, but he had his own money from his share of the ranch and also Maddie had her income from the boutique.

Joe asked, "How are you doin' on those investments?"

"Fine, but it won't last forever," Jake said.

"Talk to Tom Sebastian, but if I were you, I'd sell whatever you can right now. He handles all of our stuff now, too, so I'll be doing the same thing. I got a bad feeling that things are only gonna get worse. There's gonna be a lot places out of business, not to mention breweries and such. With all these boys comin' home from the war lookin' for work and all, the economy is gonna take a big hit. You mark my words."

Knowing Joe had his eye on such things, Jake didn't take his friend's advice lightly. "Ok. I'll do that when I leave here."

"We're gonna figure something out, Jake. There's gotta be something we can do with that place to make money. We've come up with creative solutions in the past and we will this time, too," Joe said with more heart than he felt right at the moment. He wanted to bolster Jake's spirits as much as he could.

"Wait a minute!" Jake shouted, startling Joe. "Just because we can't sell alcohol doesn't mean we have to shut down. People can still come to dance. We might not get as many customers, but it'll be better than nothing. We can still serve sarsaparilla and punch. The place is free and clear now, so there's no mortgage to worry about, either. We can still make some sort of profit."

A grin spread across Joe's features. "Yeah! Great idea! We'll have to see whether it's worth staying open on Tuesdays and Wednesdays. It'll depend on how big a crowd we get those nights. We'll keep Reckless and Patch on as bouncers. Rick doesn't need the money; Reckless and Patch do."

Jake said, "I hate to lay Brody off, but I won't do that to Reckless. He's been with us too long. And Patch doesn't have any family to fall back on the way Brody does."

"Oh, I hate this crap!" Joe shouted. "Havin' to pick and choose who gets to keep their job. I haven't had to do that for years, but it might be comin'. You're right, though. Patch is on his own and needs that job."

"Yeah. I'm keeping us closed for tonight," Jake said. "I'll get Andy to help me write up an ad for the newspaper announcing that we're just strictly a dance hall now. We'll reopen on Thursday and see how it goes. I'm gonna go tell everyone."

Joe said, "Save yourself some trouble. Go see Tom and I'll call around and set up a meeting for tonight with our gang. I'll go talk to Brody privately, though. I don't want to tell him in front of everyone. It'll be hard enough on the both of us as it is."

"Ok," Jake responded. "Make it for seven."

Joe nodded a little absently as Jake left and then went to spread the disturbing news.

The supper table was quiet that night. For most of the people assembled there, the Watering Hole had figured prominently in their lives. All five of Joe and Lacey's kids had gone there when they were little for short visits with Jake and the bouncers. Of course, if Lacey hadn't been with Joe and he got talking with someone, the kids had been good at sneaking off to observe a card game or play on the stage.

All manner of celebrations had been held there over the years and it would be a huge loss for the community if it couldn't be kept going in some form or another.

Edwina, Randall's wife, spoke up. "Joe, I know this may sound like a crazy idea, but I'm going to suggest it anyway."

Joe smiled at her. "Go ahead. I like crazy ideas."

"Not only do you own the Watering Hole building itself, but you own a lot of land around it," she said. "You'd have to check into the specifications, but it could be turned into a golf course. The sport is starting to take off now and women enjoy it as well as men. The Watering Hole could double as a club house during the day and a dance hall at night."

Joe tried not to laugh, but he couldn't hold it in. A loud guffaw escaped him and several other people laughed. However, when his mirth subsided, he said, "I'm laughing, but you might be onto something, Edie. I've heard that golf is gettin' more popular, too. It wouldn't cost us much to dig some holes, I guess. I've never played it, but I'm sure Randy has. Old Randy, I mean," he said and then cringed when he realized how that had sounded.

Randall arched an eyebrow at him. "I may be old, but I could beat you at golf any day. I'm very rusty, of course, but I still remember how to play."

"That wasn't the way I meant that and you know it," Joe said. "I guess I'll have to call you Randall whenever Randy is around. Randall." He and the butler looked at each other.

Joe said, "Naw, I can't do it," at the same time Randall said, "Please don't, Joseph."

Edwina said, "I can gather some information for you about what it would take to start a course. I can also help with creating some advertisements. You might want to think about serving simple lunches Fridays through Sundays."

"We're not gonna be open on Sundays, Edie. We never have been before," Joe said.

Edwina said, "The Watering Hole has never been closed before, either. Golf courses are open on Sundays, Joe. If you want the bar to stay open, you might have to change some other things."

Joe sighed. "You're right. I'll talk to everyone about it tonight. Why don't you come so you can answer questions about that?"

"I'd be happy to," Edwina said.

"Daddy, I have an idea, too," Tim said.

Joe's shoulders sagged. "You're talkin' about pool tables, aren't you?"

Tim nodded. "Yeah, but you should also have a small cover charge. People will come to dance, but without booze to buy, you're not gonna sell enough other drinks to make any money. Have Reckless or Patch watch the pool games and charge per game, too."

Jasmine said, "You should sell cigarettes, Pappy. I hear they're big business."

"Jasmine!" Emily objected. "I don't want you to talk about such things. Where did you hear that?"

Joe laughed. "Yeah, where'd you hear that?"

"One of the boys at school was talking about how his pa said he always runs out of cigarettes at the bar and has to borrow from someone else and then give them back."

"I see, but your mama's right; you're too little to talk about that kind of stuff. Well, between all your ideas, we might be able to keep the place open," Joe said.

Edwina said, "If there are golf enthusiasts in the towns around here, you might pull weekend business from there, too."

Lacey said, "I'll tell you what: while you and Joe go to the meeting, the rest of us will keep coming up with ideas, even if they seem silly. Then tomorrow we can go over them and see what might work."

"That's a great idea, honey," Joe said.

By the end of the meal, all of them felt more optimistic about the fate of the Watering Hole.

Chapter Thirteen

Horrific screaming made Switch and Hope bolt up in bed that night. It was Renee. Switch sped from their room, followed closely by Hope. They collided with Skip and Jethro in the hallway. It would have been comical if it had been for any other reason. In his haste to get to his daughter, Switch shoved the boys aside, rushing to Renee's bed. He sat down and gathered her to him.

"It's all right. Pa's got you, honey. It's ok," he said, rocking her.

Renee clung to him, her body shaking with terror. "They were here. Right by my bed. I don't know where they went, but they were here."

"It was just a dream," Switch said. "They're not here. You're safe. It was just a dream."

Hope also sat on the bed. "You've got three strong men here with you, sweetie. You're completely safe. Here, take a little of this."

Renee took the laudanum and rested back in the bed. "I'll be all right now. I'm sorry for disturbing all of you."

Jethro said, "No need to be sorry, sis. We're here to help you."

Skip said, "That's right. Move over."

"What are you doing?" Renee said, smiling.

"I'm gonna stay with you for the rest of the night. We used to do this all the time," Skip said.

She giggled, but then shifted over so that he could climb in with her. When he lay down, they looked at each other and laughed. The others smiled and Switch said, "You're a little big for that now, but I think we'll make an exception." *Anything to chase the nightmares away.*

Jethro left the room and returned with the bedroll he'd been sleeping on in his old room, which had been converted into a costume room. "Might as well make it a sleepover," he said, spreading the bedroll out.

Renee said, "You don't have to do that."

"I want to."

When Renee yawned, Switch and Hope kissed her goodnight and left her in the care of her brothers.

Switch and Hope lay awake in their bed, however, unable to sleep.

"I'm really proud of the boys," Hope said.

"Yeah. I'm glad that our kids have always gotten along for the most part, unlike other families," Switch said.

Hope laid her head on his chest and he held her. "I'm so worried about her, Switch. She's been so brave, but I think it's really starting to hit her now."

"I know. I wondered when it would. That's not something you just recover from quickly."

Hope sighed. "No, it's not. All we can do is what we're doing." She chuckled. "Skip is so funny, climbing in bed with Renee like that. Did you see her face light up, though? And I could tell that she was happy to have Jethro there, too."

"Yeah. They're good brothers."

"Mmm hmm," she mumbled.

Switch smiled at her sleepy response and fell silent, letting her get some sleep since she had to work the next day. He was wide awake now, which wasn't unusual for him, but he didn't get up the way he usually did. He stayed there, holding his wife and remaining vigilant in case Renee needed him.

Renee not only had nightmares, flashbacks often took her by surprise. She was afraid to leave the house and only went on short walks with one or more other people. Black Fox came to see her almost every day and he'd brought her a dream catcher for over her bed. She already had one that he'd made for her a number of years ago, but he said that an extra one couldn't hurt.

Jethro had had to return to New York even though he hated to go. She'd insisted, saying that she wasn't going to be the cause of his career suffering. Someone also stayed with her at night, including Tim, who used Jethro's bedroll. Switch and Hope didn't object because they completely trusted him and they knew that nothing untoward would occur between him and Renee.

Tim also urged Renee to do things during the day to keep herself occupied. She was physically healed by the middle of May, but the emotional strain was taking a toll on her. She was tired because of her sleep being disturbed so much and it was hard taking naps.

Tim tried to do everything in his power to help her, but there was only so much he could do, which frustrated him. He wished that he could reach into her mind and pluck out all of the terrible memories that tormented her.

Renee had unexpected visitors one day. Emily and Minx, Reckless' sister, came to see her.

Once they were seated in the parlor, Emily said, "Tim's told us what a hard time you're having and we want to help you. We both know what you're going through. Now, in my case, it wasn't as bad for me as it was for you, but it was still traumatic and I suffered terrible nightmares the same way you are."

Minx said, "I was raped by a soldier when I was eighteen winters old. It is not an easy thing to deal with. We wanted you to know that you are not alone and that you can talk to us whenever you need to. Sometimes talking with someone who has had the same thing happen to you helps a great deal."

Renee's eyes filled with tears. "I didn't know that you'd been raped,

Minx. I've heard the story about your experience, Emily, and I'm sorry that all three of us have this in common."

Renee hadn't been able to relate the whole experience in detail before, but she felt safe enough in the presence of the other women that she told them the complete story of what had happened. Minx and Emily moved over to the sofa with her, each holding one of her hands while she spoke. She shook and cried as the words poured forth. By the time she'd finished, she was exhausted, but she felt lighter.

Skip came home from school, bringing Joey and Snow Song with them, and the two women left then, promising to come see Renee again soon. Renee was glad that her other friends weren't awkward around her and they had a lively conversation about the upcoming school graduation. As long as she had people around, Renee was able to fight off the intense fear and horrible memories, but as soon as she was alone, the terror returned.

That night, Tim stayed with her and the nightmare came to her, waking her with a start. Looking towards the window, she saw them standing there and let out a whimper. Thankfully, they faded away and there was only the window once again.

"Renee?"

Tim's voice startled her and she jumped.

"Hey, it's ok. It's just me," he said, sitting up.

Fury gripped her, searing through Renee like a white-hot flame. "Go home, Tim."

"Huh? Why?"

"Because you can't keep staying with me. Everyone needs to get on with their lives, including me. I can't keep hiding away like this, expecting people to sleep on my floor or in my chair! People can't stay home with me and I need to go back to work. It's been long enough," she said.

Tim said, "Honey, you'll get back to all of that, but—"

"No, Tim. This ends now. I won't have it. I won't give them the satisfaction of cowering any longer. I'm going back to work tomorrow and you need to sleep in your own bed from now on. Everyone does," she said, her voice rising.

"Easy, Renee. How about we just see how you do with staying by yourself before you go back to work?" Tim suggested. "I understand—"

"You *don't* understand, Tim. I love you and you've been nothing but kind, loving, and supportive, but you'll never understand what I've been through," she said. "I'm not *me*, Tim, and I miss me. You don't know what it's like to lose yourself. I need to find that woman again. So, after tonight, no more sleepovers, and I'm going back to work and going back to my apartment," she said.

"You can't," Tim said.

"Yes, I can. You watch me. I'll be all right," she said.

Tim shook his head. "You can't because Mrs. Bissinger rented it to someone else. She needed the money, so she rented it again. I offered to pay your rent and so did your pa, but she wants someone living in the apartment and we didn't know when you'd be able to go back."

"See!" she shouted. "They took that from me, too!"

"Shh! We'll find you another place when the time is right," Tim said.

"I will not be quiet! No one will keep me silent! When Mitch finds them, I'm going to testify and tell the whole world what they did to me. Every ghastly, vile thing," Renee said, sitting up.

The rest of her family came to her room.

Renee grew angrier. "Go back to bed! And you need to leave," she said to Tim. "I can stay on my own now. I'll be fine. I'm going to work in the morning, too. I'm going to get my life back. I'll go back to work and find a little place again."

Hope said, "Honey, I don't think you should be so hasty."

"I need to. I'll be in at my usual time," Renee announced. The room fell silent and she looked around at them all as understanding dawned. "My job is gone, isn't it? You hired someone else? How could you do that?"

"I didn't want to, Renee, but we had to. We've been so busy lately and we needed someone to do the work," Hope said. Guilt and anguish filled her eyes.

Renee's hands fisted in her nightgown and she looked down at it.

Sudden hatred for the garment rose up. “They’ve taken my apartment, which I loved. They’ve taken my job, which I loved, but they won’t take anything else. I swear to God, they won’t take anything else. And I will never wear another nightgown again. Do you know why? I couldn’t get away because my legs got tangled up in it. If I hadn’t been wearing it, I could have made it to the kitchen. I could have reached the knives. Maybe I wouldn’t have killed them, but I could have wounded them. At least my chances would have been better.”

Switch said, “Renee, let’s not discuss that right now.”

“And you,” she said, fixing him with a glare filled with loathing. “You accused me of being a whore.”

“I did not,” Switch said.

“Oh, yes, you did. You warned men away from me because you thought I was sleeping with anything in pants. I guess you found out otherwise, didn’t you? I’m sure Marcus told you that I was a virgin until the night those animals raped me,” Renee said.

Switch stepped closer. “Renee, I’ve apologized for that, but I never thought you were a whore. I was overprotective, but—”

Renee launched herself off the bed at him, but Tim interceded, wrapping his arms around her from behind to prevent her from attacking Switch.

“Get out of my sight,” she hurled at Switch. “Get away from me! You probably think this was my fault. That’s what people think. I did something to encourage them. I deserved what I got. Isn’t that right?”

“No! Never! I would never think anything like that!” Switch said.

“Yes, you did!”

“Renee, you have to calm down,” Tim said.

Hope tugged on Switch’s arm. “Switch, just leave for now. It’ll be all right.”

“But I can’t have her thinking such a thing about me.”

Skip said, “Pa, c’mon.”

Switch looked at his son and then back at Renee. The hate in her eyes broke his heart and he knew it was useless to talk to her any more. He’d lost her. Numbly, he walked from the room, going to his own. He stood there for a moment before going back out into the hallway. He heard the other three trying to calm Renee down.

He went downstairs, put on his shoes and jacket, and went out into the cool night in only his long underwear.

Black Fox looked at the lone figure in the distance and sighed in relief and sadness. He walked across the canyon where his tribe had stayed for a couple of years before the military had found them and forced them onto the reservation. It was also where his first wife, Wind Spirit, had been laid to rest when she'd succumbed to meningitis.

He felt the spirits of many of his departed loved ones here in the canyon, where they'd been buried, including his brother He Who Runs' and sister-in-law, Eagle Woman's. They'd been killed in the bloody battle that night. Thrusting those memories away, the chief instead concentrated on the reason he'd come.

Sitting down by Switch, he put a hand on his shoulder. "You have been here for the past two days?"

"Yeah. I can't go home and I knew if I went anywhere else, people would just try to make me," Switch said. "She hates me, Black Fox. My little girl hates me."

"She does not hate you. She is beside herself with anger and grief right now and does not know what to do with it all. Your wife and other people have been worried about you."

"I'm sorry about that, but if I go home, it'll upset Renee even more and I can't take seeing the hate in her eyes," Switch said.

Black Fox said, "Being the father of a hurting child is not easy, especially when it is the heart that is wounded."

"You're not kidding. I can see why she'd think what she does, but it really wasn't like that," Switch said. "You see how beautiful she is and I see the way men look at her. Black Fox, I did what I did because I didn't want her to get hurt. I didn't want something like what happened to happen.

You have to understand something and I don't know how I'm ever going to explain it to her."

"I am listening."

"Renee has exhibited risky behavior in the past. I know this because I had the fathers of two different boys tell me that they'd caught their son and Renee in rather compromising situations. The boys had been severely dealt with in each case. I told Hope about it and we talked to Renee about allowing boys to take advantage of her like that.

"We thought she understood, but a couple of years later, I heard a couple of young men at the bar talking about her. That's when I started warning men away from her. I figured that if she lacked impulse control the way I had, then I would try to control the situation another way," Switch said.

"I see. That is a hard situation, especially now that she is an adult," Black Fox responded. "You cannot keep doing that, but I understand why you want to."

"The boys she'd been caught with wouldn't say anything either way if things had actually gone too far and Renee wouldn't tell Hope if they had or not. We hoped, but we didn't know that she'd still ... been ... pure." He struggled to get the words out. "Not until Marcus told Hope and me that she had been until she was attacked."

Black Fox closed his eyes, thinking about Minx, who'd also had her virginity violently stolen. "I can see now why you would be so protective of her. It seems that no matter how protective we are, though, bad things happen to our children. You love Renee very much and only wanted to help her."

Switch let out a sarcastic laugh. "Yeah, but it backfired. That's why she moved out in the first place. She found out about what I'd been doing and got mad at me. So she moved out. I tried to convince her to stay at home, but she wouldn't."

"You're a smart man, Switch. Crazy, but smart."

Switch smiled a little. "So I've been told."

"This is not your fault. Do not let guilt stop you from doing what

Renee needs you to do. There is no way anyone could have known this would happen. Children grow up and leave home. Renee needs you to make her see how much you love her," Black Fox said.

"How can I do that when she doesn't want to see me?" Switch said. "How can I do that when she hates me?"

"She does not hate you. You are just where she is focusing her anger. You must wait until her anger fades. Then you will be able to explain things to her. If you stay away, she will think that she is right in thinking you thought badly of her," Black Fox said. "You must not let that happen. Your daughter needs you, and even though it will be the hardest thing you have ever done, you must stay strong in the face of her anger. If you can survive your parents, you can survive this."

Switch met his eyes. "You're right. She's my daughter and I can't fail her. I always promised myself that if I ever did have kids someday, I would never let them down the way my parents let me down. I'm gonna keep that promise to myself, but more importantly to them." He jumped up and Black Fox rose with him. "Thanks, Chief."

"You are welcome."

Switch hugged Black Fox and ran off, intent on getting home to his family.

Chapter Fourteen

Renee was sitting at the kitchen table reading the newspaper when Switch arrived home. She looked up at him but didn't speak.

He forced a small smile onto his face. "I know you're really angry with me and that's ok. If being mad at me helps you, then so be it, but I hope you won't stay mad at me forever so I can talk to you about some things. And no matter how angry you are at me, I'll always love you. I'm your father and I'll always be here for you, no matter what. Ok, I'm going to clean up and change and put on more than underwear. I stink." As he passed behind her, he pressed a quick kiss to the top of her head.

Renee was still angry with Switch and didn't want to spend the day around him, but where was she going to go? Could she go out on her own? There was only one way to find out. She wanted to go to Elliot's to buy some boys' underwear, figuring that she would be able to find something to fit her. She'd borrowed some from Skip, but they'd been too big.

She put on her jacket and took a deep breath. "You can do this, Renee. You're a good actress, so just walk along pretending everything is fine and it will be."

Making it to the sidewalk in front of her house, she stood for several minutes gathering her courage. Then she made it across the street and did the same thing, willing her heart to settle down so she could continue on her way. In a series of short walks, she reached Main Street. It seemed a lifetime since she'd walked along the street.

People walked past her, some speaking to her. Renee returned pleasantries, even as she saw pity in their eyes. They would never say anything to her face, but she knew that they would talk about her later on. Some people would think that she'd brought her attack on herself, but she couldn't worry about them. It was time to regain her life.

She stopped walking when she neared the Shutter Shoppe. Looking up, she saw the windows to her apartment and experienced a flashback. Trembling, she closed her eyes, forcing herself to calm down. "They're not here. You're strong and there's nothing to be afraid of," she whispered. "Now go to Elliot's and buy some damn underwear!"

"Renee?"

She opened her eyes to see Tim standing before her with an uncertain expression on his face. "Hello, Timmy," she said, smiling at him.

"Hi. Are you all right?" he asked.

"No, but I'm pretending I am," she said. "And the more I pretend, the quicker I will be. I'm going to buy some boys' underwear come hell or high water."

Tim's mouth curved with amusement at her feisty statement. "All right. May I come along on this underwear shopping? I can help you pick some out since I'm a boy."

"How do you always know what I need? Yes, I would love for you to escort me," she said.

He offered his arm to her and as she took it, Renee remembered how they'd done that so many times. She felt more darkness slip away, letting a little more light back into her soul.

"Does Skip need underwear?" Tim asked.

"No, I do. I told you that I wasn't going to ever wear a nightgown again and I meant it. I don't want to wear pantalets to bed, so I'm buying boys' underwear," Renee said.

Before he thought about it, Tim said, "Damn. I wish I was still staying over with you so you could model them for me." Realizing how that sounded, he stopped walking. "I'm sorry, Renee. I'm just so used to being playful with you like that."

Renee grinned at him. "I'm glad you said it. I need that, Tim. I need us to get back to the way we used to be. I feel completely safe with you. Please don't walk on eggshells with me. Not anymore."

"Anything for you, Snuggle Bunny," he said softly as they started walking again.

She squeezed his arm and giggled. "I've missed you calling me that."

"I've missed calling you that," he said.

"Well, I better hear it from now on, Mr. Dwyer," she said.

"Yes, ma'am."

Buying underwear with Tim was a hilarious affair and did Renee a world of good. She looked at union long underwear, but it would be a pain to have to unbutton everything when she needed to do her business, so she bought several sets of B.V.D. undershirts and knee-length drawers.

As they left the store, Tim asked, "Can this lowly cowboy buy you dinner this evening at the Grady House?"

"I would be delighted to dine with you, but there's nothing lowly about you. You're my knight in shining armor."

"Pick you up at six?"

"Six it is, and if you hear of anyone hiring, please let me know. I need a job and to keep getting back to normal."

Tim stopped walking. "Are you sure you're ready? I've been really worried about you since the other night."

"I'm so sorry about all of that, Tim. It was so awful and I'm so sorry I put you through it. It was like all of this anger was trapped inside. I felt like a volcano and I finally exploded."

"It's all right, honey. Please don't worry about it."

She nodded. "All right."

"Do you want me to take you home? I brought a buggy," he said.

"No. I appreciate the offer, but I need to be able to go places by myself and you need to let me go by myself. No one can be with me all the time, Tim," she said. She rose on tiptoe to kiss his cheek. "I'll see you tonight, handsome."

"Ok. I'll see you tonight," he said. As she walked away, Tim desperately wished that he was going with her. Only when she turned the corner, walking out of sight, did he get in his buggy and drive away.

—෴—

Eating out that night made Renee nervous, but she was able to get through their meal thanks to Tim's attentiveness and his holding her hand. His touch helped dispel her anxiety. When they were done, she asked to go for a drive and he was happy to comply. After driving around for a while, he took her home.

He hugged her close, reveling in the way she felt in his arms. "I love you."

She snuggled against him. "I love you, too."

They stayed that way for a little while before he pulled away. I'll walk you in," he said.

Renee laid her hand against his jaw. "Timmy, please kiss me."

"Are you sure?"

"Yes. I need to know you still want me," she said.

"I'll always want you, Renee."

Lowering his head, he brushed his mouth against hers before kissing her more firmly. Renee closed her eyes and forced away her fears. This was her Tim she was kissing, the man who'd captured her heart and made her feel loved and respected. The man who excited her and made her burn with need. Winding her arms around his neck, she kissed him back, answering his silent question by moving closer to him.

It had been so long since he'd kissed Renee like this that it was hard to hold his passion in check, but he forced himself to go slow. He never wanted to do anything to frighten her. She meant too much to him to rush. Her slightly vanilla scent was delicious, as were her soft lips. Holding her closer, he kissed her a little harder, a small moan escaping him.

Renee answered with one of her own and pressed harder against him, loving the way his powerful arms held her and the heat he created inside her. She felt him begin to pull away and the kiss ended. She noticed that his eyes had darkened with desire and that his chest rose and fell a little harder than normal. Her hands rested on his chest and she ran them over his hard muscles.

"I wanted you to be my first, Timmy. I wanted to give myself to you, but now that's gone," she said, tears welling in her eyes.

He kissed them away when they spilled over. "I will be. What happened wasn't lovemaking, honey. I'll still be your first." *Your one and only if I have my way.*

Her gaze held his. "You want to make love to me after what happened? You're not … repulsed by me?"

An intense expression settled on his handsome features. "If you repulsed me, would I kiss you like this?"

Even though he moved slowly, the kiss he gave her was desire-filled and left them both breathless.

"I guess not," she said.

He smiled and blew out a breath. "Lord, what you do to me. We'd better go in."

Renee agreed and they walked up the walkway holding hands.

A few nights later, Tim picked up Renee for dinner, but they didn't go to any of the restaurants in town.

"Where are we going?" Renee asked.

"You'll see," Tim said with a mysterious smile.

Renee bounced on her seat a little. "I love surprises."

"Good. Oh, and Jake wants to meet with you tomorrow at one to discuss a job he has available," Tim said.

Her eyes lit up. "Really? As what?"

"A waitress. Roberta quit. Do you think you'd like it? There's no pressure on you to take it, but I guess he thought of you right away," Tim explained.

"I think that would be so fun," she said. "I'm glad they still have enough business to stay open."

"The cover charge and pool tables combined with the drinks really help. Will it bother you to be around that many people?"

"No," she said, forcing away her fear. "I'll be just fine."

"Ok. I think you're a great fit for the job, plus you'll probably make out good on tips," he said.

He turned left onto a less-used road and Renee recognized it as the one leading to the Dwyer family cabin. She asked him again what he was up to, but he refused to tell her. Going inside, she saw that there was already a fire going in the large hearth in the great room. Tim lit a couple of lamps and she saw her phonograph player sitting off to the side.

At her questioning look, Tim said, "I thought you might like to do some dancing."

"I would love to dance," she said.

Tim took her hand and twirled her around. "Then dance we shall. Go put on whatever you'd like. I just have to check on dinner."

"You cooked?" Now that he mentioned it, she smelled something delicious.

He nodded. "Yes, I did. I'll be right back."

Going over to the player, Renee picked out a song and cranked the player to life. Tim returned.

"Dinner will be a little while, so we have time for a few dances," he said, taking her in his arms.

As they danced, they talked and laughed. Renee felt freer than she had in a long time as they moved around the room. They were well matched and danced well together. When it was time, Tim finished getting dinner ready.

"Come on in the kitchen," he called to her.

Entering the room, she smiled upon seeing the candlelit table, which had been covered by a checkered cloth. Tim seated her.

"What did you do?" she asked.

"Something nice," he replied, pulling a baking dish from the oven. "I hope you're hungry. Think you can eat some stuffed shells and garlic bread?"

"I'm starving and that smells heavenly," she said. "Hurry up."

He laughed. "Yes, ma'am."

Once he'd dished up the food, Renee savored the tangy, cheesy meal. Watching her enjoy the food made Tim feel good. He wanted to do special things for her and show her how much she meant to him. Once they'd finished, Renee insisted on helping him clean up and it was nice doing such a domestic thing together.

"Would you like to dance some more?" he asked.

"I'd love to."

Tim put a song on and wrapped his arms around Renee. "Do you have any idea how happy you make me?"

Not meeting his eyes, Renee said, "I'm sure I haven't made you happy for a while now."

He lifted her chin "That's not true. Yes, I've been worried about you and I've been so angry about what they did to you, but I'm always happy when I'm with you. I love everything about you: your smile, the way your eyes shine when you laugh, and your naughty sense of humor. You're the most beautiful woman in the world and I can't imagine my life without you. I love you so much. Will you make me even happier by becoming my wife, Renee?"

Renee gasped and stopped dancing. "Did you just ask me to marry you?"

"Yes. Will you marry me?"

Light and joy flooded her being and she felt as though she were floating. "I would love to become your wife. Yes, I'll marry you!" She threw her arms around him and kissed him.

Happiness so powerful that it almost took his breath away swelled inside Tim and he kissed her with abandon. When they finally broke apart, Tim put a splendid, shimmering diamond on her finger.

Gazing intently at her, he said, "You're mine forever now."

"And you're mine." Renee gave him a saucy smile. "Close your eyes."

With a questioning glance, he asked, "Why? What are you up to?"

"You'll see. Turnabout is fair play. No peeking."

Grinning, he closed his eyes. Listening closely, he tried to figure out what she was doing, but he couldn't.

"You can open your eyes now."

When he did, shock reverberated through him. Renee stood wearing nothing but the boy's underwear she'd bought. Tim had never thought a woman wearing men's underwear could be alluring, but Renee was. The sleeveless shirt showed off her pretty arms, shoulders, and neck. She filled the shirt out in a way a man never could and the knee-length trousers clung to her hips and left her shapely thighs and calves bared to his eyes.

Hunger ripped through him. "Oh, God, Renee. You're gorgeous."

"You said you wanted to see them. I take it that you like them," she said a little shyly. Although she was a little nervous about showing so much of herself to him, she still felt safe with Tim. She would have never done this with anyone else, not after that terrible night.

"I love them. I feel overdressed," he said.

She sent him a wicked little grin. "Well, I'm sure you can remedy that."

His eyebrows knitted together. "Are you sure? I don't want to scare you."

"If you were scaring me, I wouldn't suggest such a thing."

A smile spread across his face and he unbuttoned his shirt, letting it drop to the floor. He loosened his belt, giving her a questioning look. Renee smiled and motioned that he was to keep going. His jeans joined his shirt and he stood wearing much the same thing she was, but he filled the underwear out in a completely different way.

Renee's eyes traveled over him from head to toe, drinking in his strong shoulders and arms, powerful chest, and muscular thighs. Desire flared to life and she stepped closer to him, running her hands up his arms. His eyes smoldered with passion and he couldn't keep his hands off her.

"Dance with me," he said, trailing his fingers down her arms.

She giggled. "I'd love to."

Dancing with each other in their underwear was fun, naughty, and arousing, but as much as he wanted her, Tim would hold himself in check forever if necessary. Renee appreciated his restraint, but she was ready to give herself to the man who would become her husband.

The song ended and Renee said, "Please make love with me, Timmy. I need you to show me how it's supposed to feel. I want to show you how much I love you. Please?"

Her heartfelt plea made it impossible to resist her. He answered her by kissing her long and slow, nibbling on her bottom lip and running his fingers into her silky hair. Slowly, he drew back from her and picked her up. As he carried her upstairs, his eyes barely left hers. It hadn't been his intention to make love to her that night, but he knew that he would have no regrets about it.

He took her to the room he always used and set her on her feet. "Are you absolutely sure?"

She reached out, quickly undoing the buttons on his under shirt. "More than sure." She spread the shirt open, her nostrils flaring slightly at the sight of his manly chest.

He sucked in a breath as she slid her hands up to his shoulders. "I won't do anything you're not comfortable with and we'll take our time. I'm not in a rush. I want to show you how much I love you, too, and how beautiful you are. I *am* your first, Renee, your true first, and I'm going to be the only man you'll ever make love with again."

His possessiveness heightened her excitement and she rose up, pressing her lips against his. With exquisite tenderness, Tim took her on a sensual journey, and when she became nervous, he eased her anxiety with loving words and sweet kisses. Renee wasn't afraid of Tim at all, rather she was concerned that she wouldn't please him and it was extremely important to her that she did.

She needn't have worried. Everything about Renee excited Tim and being with her was the most powerful, moving experience of his life. As he loved her, he knew that his craving for her would never be satisfied and he was glad that they would have a lifetime together.

In Tim's arms, Renee felt her soul and heart healing even more and she rejoiced over the miracle of Tim's love. He was more than she could have ever dreamed of and she gave herself completely to him that night, knowing that she would always be safe and happy with him.

Chapter Fifteen

Tim hated to wake Renee, but it was getting late and he didn't want her parents to get worried about her—or to suspect anything had gone on between them other than becoming engaged. He kissed her shoulder and tightened his arm around her.

"Renee, it's getting late, honey."

She made a sound of protest. "I don't want to go. I just want to stay here with you forever."

He smiled. "I'd love that, too, but I have to get you home before they send a search party after you."

Rolling over, she gave him a drowsy smile and caressed his cheek. "I've never felt anything so wonderful. Thank you for loving me and for showing me how beautiful lovemaking is meant to be. I don't know how, but I love you even more than before."

"I feel the same way," Tim said, holding her closer. "I love you more than I ever thought I could possibly love someone. I can't wait to marry you."

"Well, let's start planning right away." She sighed and got out of bed.

Tim averted his eyes from her lush curves, knowing that if he looked at her too long, he would haul her back into bed. Once they were dressed, they made sure everything was straightened up and left. On the drive back to town, they didn't say much. Renee sat close to Tim and whenever the road allowed him to drive one-handed, he put an arm around her.

He walked her to the door, giving her a lingering kiss. They didn't say goodbye. Their gazes locked and their eyes did all of their talking. Tim kissed her forehead and went back to his car. Renee watched him go and then went inside. She felt different—more womanly and happier than she'd ever been.

A lamp burned in the parlor and she knew it was her father who was up so late. Indecision gripped her. Should she talk to him? Guilt for the way she'd treated him set in and she thought that it was time to hear him out. When she walked into the parlor, he looked up and smiled at her.

"Hi, honey. For the record, I was not waiting up for you. I'm just having one of those nights. I was looking over some of this financial stuff, but it's not making much sense to me. Tom says we should sell some stock because the market is unstable right now and blah, blah, blah. I just give him money and he invests it for me. I don't have the foggiest idea of how that all works. I've tried to figure it out, but it just gets all mixed up in my mind, which isn't surprising. Anyway, you don't want to hear about all of that."

Renee couldn't help smiling at his rambling explanation as she sat on the sofa. She was careful to hide her left hand, intending to tell everyone about becoming engaged all at once in the morning. "It's all right, Pa. I want to apologize for the way I've acted towards you and the hateful things I said to you. It wasn't right and I'm sorrier than I can really say."

Switch put aside his papers and sat forward. "It's ok, honey. You needed an outlet and I was willing to be that for you. I won't pretend it didn't hurt, but I understand. I need to explain to you why I did what I did, because I have good reasons for doing it, although maybe I could have done it a different way or talked to you or something."

"Pa."

"I'm doing it again. Ok. Sorry. See, when I was your age, I had no self-control where women were concerned, and I was pretty popular with the ladies."

Renee let out a snort of laughter. "You?"

He frowned. "Yes, me. Why does everyone have such a hard time believing that? When I turn on the charm, there are very few women who can refuse me. Ask your mother. Plus women like guys who make them laugh. Doesn't Tim make you laugh?"

She smiled. "Yes."

"And isn't there a certain look he gives you that makes you feel warm inside?"

"Yes."

"Right. There are some men who know how to do that and some that don't. I'm one of the ones who does."

Renee grinned. "My father, the Casanova."

"That's right. Anyhow, I don't need to go into all the stuff with my parents, but when I was with a woman, I felt good about myself for a little while. I think that's one reason why I didn't have much control. Do you remember when Hope and I had that talk with you about those boys?"

Renee's face colored. "Yes. I'll never forget that."

"Me, neither. Look, my biggest fear about having kids was that I would pass my craziness on to them; I did in Skip's case, which I feel really bad about. You're so beautiful and I see the way men watch you. I was worried that I may have passed on my lack of willpower to you. Maybe that's stupid, but that's what I was afraid of. I overheard those men talking about you like you were some piece of meat ..." He trailed off, staring into space. "Renee!" He jumped up. "It might be them! One was average height, sort of pudgy with a reddish beard. You said that you saw a little bit of the one's face and he had a brown or red beard."

Renee stood up with him, gripping his arm, hope and dread surging through her at once. "Yes. And he had a small scar at the base of his throat."

Switch frowned. "I don't know if he had a scar, but he had sort of a gravelly voice."

Her hand tightened on his arm. "Yes! Almost like he was hoarse."

Switch sat her down on the sofa with him. "And the other one was taller and he had an odd laugh. Like a coughing sound?"

Renee closed her eyes, forcing herself to envision the men and listen to them. She grabbed Switch's hand, needing the contact to avoid giving in to panic. Opening her eyes, she looked into his and nodded. "Yes. I don't know how I could think about such a thing at the time, but I remember thinking that he must have a cold. I guess I was trying to focus on something other than …"

A fury unlike any that she'd ever seen shone in Switch's eyes and it was a little scary to behold. He hadn't even looked like that the night that a guy had pushed her at the Watering Hole. The sheer rage in his expression was startling.

"If I find out it was them—"

She squeezed his hand harder. "No, Pa. Don't do anything. I need you here, not in jail. And I need to face them and put them behind bars. Please don't deny me that."

Some of the anger left him. "You're right. I think the shorter guy's last name was Parsons. He called the other one Bret."

"They never called each other by name," Renee said. "But they sound like the same guys."

"We'll go tell Mitch right away in the morning."

In their excitement, Renee forgot to hide her left hand. Switch caught the glint of her diamond in the lamplight. He grabbed her hand and looked at the fine ring.

"Holy Hannah!" he shouted. "Is that what I think it is?"

Renee giggled. "Yes, it is. Tim asked me to marry him and I accepted."

"Hot damn! We need to celebrate." He ran out to the kitchen, retrieved two cups and a bottle of rum, and brought them back into the parlor. "You wanna know how stupid the government is about this whole prohibition stuff?"

"How stupid are they?" Renee asked, taking the cup he handed her.

"You can't make, sell, transport, or store booze, but there's nothing in the law that says you can't drink it. Isn't that stupid? Of course, I guess they figure that if you can't do all of those things, there's no way for people to consume it, but you just watch; people are gonna get it one way or another. Moonshiners are gonna make a fortune selling their booze," Switch said. "To my little girl getting engaged to the man of her dreams."

They touched their cups and took a swallow of rum. Both of them made faces of distaste and then laughed at each other. Footsteps sounded on the stairs and Skip came in, squinting in the lamplight.

"What are you guys doing?" he asked.

"Sorry for waking you, Skippy," Renee said. "We were just celebrating a little." She held out her left hand to him.

Skip's eyes bugged out. "Tim proposed? Wow! What a ring! Holy cow! I'm so happy for you," he said, giving her a hug.

Switch handed him his cup. "I don't normally give you liquor, but I'll make an exception since this is a special occasion."

Skip downed the rum and licked his lips. "Good stuff. Thanks, Pa."

Chuckling, Renee handed him her cup and he drank that, too. "That's enough now. We don't want you going to school drunk."

Skip said, "No, I want to be able to graduate next week. I don't need to get suspended or something. I'll make sure to brush my teeth real well in the morning. So Tim's gonna be my brother-in-law. How about that?"

"That's right."

Switch went to the bottom of the stairs. "We can't leave your mother out of this. She'll kill us. Hope! Honey, come here!"

In a moment, Hope appeared at the top of the stairs. "What's wrong?"

"Nothing. Come here. We have good news."

Hope came down, wondering why they were all so happy until Renee showed her the ring. She let out a shout and embraced Renee.

"Oh, honey! I'm so happy for you. You're getting a good man," Hope said. "And he's getting a good woman. I can't believe my baby girl is getting married."

"*You* can't believe it? I can't, either. I have to walk her down the aisle and give her away," Switch said, sudden tears springing into his eyes. "Just yesterday you were born and I held you for the first time and now here you are, getting engaged and ready to fly the coop." He knelt next to Renee. "Don't you see? I'm your father and there's nothing I won't do to keep you safe, even if you get mad at me. I love you so much. I've never thought anything bad about you, Renee. Not like you think I did. I promise you that."

All of Renee's anger faded away and she put her arms around Switch's neck, hugging him close. "I understand now, Pa. I'm so sorry I hurt you like that. So sorry. You've always been the best father and I should've known that you had reasons for your actions. Please forgive me."

"Of course, honey. Don't worry about it anymore. It's forgotten," he said, stroking her hair. His heart filled with happiness over reconciling with Renee, washing away the hurt.

When he'd released her and stood up, Renee said, "I have a job interview tomorrow with Jake at the Watering Hole. He'd like to hire me as a waitress. Tim said Roberta quit and I was the first person Jake thought of."

Hope didn't like the idea of Renee working there, but figured that it was safer there now since alcohol was no longer served at the bar. Plus, there were still bouncers and Jake and Andy would keep an eye on her. No matter how much she wanted to, Hope knew she couldn't keep Renee in a cocoon. "You'll be a great waitress, honey. Sounds like this interview is just a formality."

Switch nodded even though the thought of Renee working where those two men might come back terrified him. "And you know Jake and Joe pay well, too. You'll be able to get your own place again in no time. I know how bad you want to be on your own."

"I've been thinking about that since Tim proposed to me tonight. What's the sense of me moving into my own place when we're not going to wait long to get married? That would just be a waste of time and money," Renee said.

Hope said, "I think that's very practical of you." She couldn't hide her pleased smile.

Switch and Skip wore the same expressions, which made Renee laugh. "What are you going to do once Tim and I are married? I'm not going to be living here, you know."

Skip hugged her. "Yeah, but at least we have you for a while longer. How long of an engagement are you going to have? A year, two? Five?"

"Not nearly that long. We haven't discussed that yet. We just got engaged. Let us enjoy it a little," Renee said.

Their little celebration broke up then. As Renee lay down to sleep, she smiled thinking about the wonderful evening she'd spent with Tim. The nightmare came, just like always, but this time, she combatted the memory of the heinous treatment she'd received by her attackers with the new memory of the bliss she'd shared with Tim.

Instead of seeing the hideous pillowcase masks, she saw Tim's handsome smile and love-filled eyes. She fought off the cruel words the two men had said to her with the words of passion Tim had softly uttered to her. By showing Renee the pleasure a man and woman could share, Tim had given her the most powerful weapon against the evil she'd endured: love. It was that love that brought Renee through to the morning light, feeling stronger and more confident than she had since the attack had occurred.

Chapter Sixteen

Mitch listened to Switch and Renee the next morning and agreed that they were on to something, but the problem was that Renee hadn't actually seen their faces. The fact that she'd been so dazed at the time also compromised the case and they couldn't just go around accusing every man who matched her and Switch's descriptions. Although they understood his point of view, father and daughter were disheartened.

Just as they were about to leave, Mitch said, "Where are you going? There's still something we can do, but it depends on whether you're willing to do it."

They sat back down.

"Since Switch saw these two men at the bar, I'm inclined to agree with you that they probably frequent the place. Your working there would give us a great advantage, Renee. If you encounter them and you're positive that it's them, don't react to them. You let me know and we'll set up a trap. I know all about the stunts you pulled at Christmas and I think you have the talent to do this, too," Mitch said.

Renee jumped at the chance to help apprehend her assailants. "Whatever it takes to catch them and tell the whole world what they did, I'll do it."

Mitch smiled. "I'm glad you're willing to testify. A lot of women won't take the chance of public humiliation if the verdict doesn't go their way."

"Who do you think I'm doing this for?" Renee said. "I'm not only doing it for me, but for every woman who's ever been a victim of such brutality. I'm giving those women who can't speak for themselves a voice. I will have my day in court, but I'll be doing much more than testifying against two rapists; I'll be showing women everywhere that they need to stand up for themselves because sometimes no one else will stand up for you. I'm very fortunate to have family and friends who love and support me, but not all women do."

Switch gave her a sideways squeeze. "That's my brave girl. Well said, honey."

Mitch said, "I agree. We'll keep you completely safe, Renee. I guarantee that."

"I have every faith in you, Sheriff," she said, smiling.

The Kellers left, Renee's spirits high as she anticipated exacting revenge. It was time that the hunted become the hunter.

"Damn it, Hailey!" Art complained laughingly. "That ain't fair!"

She grinned at him as she pinned him down. "A warrior uses all of the weapons at their disposal."

He grinned. "So braves make a habit of kissing other braves to distract them?"

She laughed. "I haven't heard of that, but it worked on you."

Hailey made the mistake of relaxing a little and Art turned the tables on her, flipping her over and putting her in a loose chokehold with his legs wrapped around her midsection.

"Ok, Pocahontas. What're you gonna do now?"

If anyone else had called her the Indian names he did, she would have been highly offended, but Hailey knew that Art respected her and her heritage. They weren't meant to disparage her people; they were said in fun and made her laugh.

"I'll think of something," she ground out between clenched teeth.

Art soon found out what that something was when he felt her unbuckle his belt. "Hey! Don't do that unless you mean it."

Hailey broke out into loud laughter as she slid his belt from the belt loops. Art growled and let her go, snatching the belt from her hand. Quickly he secured it around his waist again.

"You're the sneakiest female I've ever come up against," he said, rising.

"I learned that from my cousin, Reckless. He did that one time in a fight against Dr. Walker when they worked as bouncers together at the bar. He won the fight," Hailey said, brushing the dust from her leggings.

Art smiled. "I would have enjoyed seeing that. All right. I gotta get to work. Where's my friendly kiss?"

Hailey wrapped her arms around his neck and looked into his eyes. "Are you coming to play cards tonight?"

"Of course I am. I'm not gonna miss the chance to beat you again." She scowled, making him laugh. "You're the only woman I know who even looks beautiful with her face all scrunched up like that."

"Shut up and kiss me."

"I do love a bossy woman," Art said before complying.

Hailey giggled against his mouth until he put his hand on the tie that would release her leggings. She stilled and pulled back from him a little. He smiled at her. "Now, you did say that a warrior uses all the weapons at his disposal, so you can't be mad at me."

She laughed again and he embraced her before giving her a real kiss. Hailey felt the familiar rush of desire and happiness she experienced whenever she kissed him. It didn't matter how he kissed her, softly lingering over her lips or fierce and wild, he always left her wanting more.

Art also wanted more—more of Hailey and to make her his wife, but he didn't know how that would be possible with the law against whites and blacks marrying. It was muddled by the fact that both of them were biracial. Would the law swing in their favor or would one or both of them wind up in jail? There were some judges who felt the whole matter was ridiculous and refused to give anyone jail time.

Then there was the fact that Matt, or any other preacher for that matter, couldn't perform the ceremony without getting in trouble. The marriage wouldn't be valid even if they did. His mind turned the problem over all day, but he didn't come up with a solution. When he arrived in camp that night, he found Raven at the central fire.

"Can I talk to you?" he asked him.

Raven rose and walked with Art to a private spot.

"I'll get right to it, Raven. I love your girl. I lost my heart to her in France and what I feel for her gets stronger every day. I want to marry her, but I can't because of that damn law," Art said. "I wanna do right by her, but how can I do that if I can't marry her?"

"Have you asked her to marry you?"

"No. I don't think she's ready for that yet, but even when she is, I can't ask her. No pastor is gonna perform the ceremony," Art said.

A sly smile spread across Raven's chiseled features. "There is one way, but it won't be recognized by the law. How do you feel about having a medicine man marry you?"

"You mean Mike?"

"Yes. He can marry you and Hailey when the time is right. I know it won't be a Christian ceremony or binding by law, but it will be binding in your hearts. Will that be enough for you?"

"You mean the way Minx and Sonny got married?"

"Yes."

"And that would be enough for you and Zoe?"

Raven nodded. "Yes. It's the way our people have done it for thousands of years. There were no pieces of paper to be signed or any priests or pastors. Our medicine men performed the ceremony, joining the two people together for as long as they wished to be. In most cases, it was a lasting relationship." He stepped closer to Art, his expression turning slightly threatening. "I'll be blunt. If you take Hailey's virginity, you will automatically become her husband and I will expect you to take her as your wife and take care of her. If you aren't prepared to do that, don't cross that line. Are we agreed?"

Art didn't back down from very many people, Raven included, but he respected Raven's right as a father to be worried about his daughter being disrespected. "Yes, sir. We're agreed."

They grasped arms and then Art went to find Hailey. Raven gazed wistfully after him, thinking that he was losing another daughter. Now he knew how his father felt over not only losing Winona to marriage, but to her choice to stay on the reservation with her new husband. Looking across the clearing to where Winona sat with Brown Otter, her second husband, he thanked Wakan Tanka for bringing her back to them.

His son, Dusty, walked across the clearing to him.

"Did he ask you for permission to marry Hailey?" he asked in Lakota.

Raven met Dusty's dark gaze. "That is none of your business."

Dusty grinned. "Which means that he did. What did you say?"

"You are as bad as Aunt Tessa," Raven teased. "I gave him permission. He is a good man and he loves her. I do not know how many other men would because she is so fierce."

"I think they are a good match, too," Dusty said, brushing his dark brown hair out of his eyes.

It was still growing out from his time in the army and it was an annoying in-between length. He'd been proud to serve his country, but he'd hated having his hair so short. He also would have preferred to have been in battle, but Dusty was a realist and knew that while he was a good fighter, his clumsiness would have tripped him up somehow. When he was sparring at home, it didn't matter, but in war there was no room for klutziness.

Walking could be a challenge to him some days and Raven suspected that Dusty needed glasses like Zoe did. However, he knew that Dusty didn't want to be the only Indian wearing glasses. He was going to talk to him about it again, but not just then.

Raven looked up at the stars, wondering if he and Zoe's youngest child, Runner, was doing the same thing. The boy had had a bad case of wanderlust and had taken off two years ago on his own version of a vision quest. He'd only been sixteen when he'd run away. He'd left a letter saying that the *Paha Sapa*, the Black Hills of South Dakota, had called to him and he needed to go see the ancient, sacred lands there. They'd searched for him, but Runner was as wily as a fox and if he didn't want to be found, he wouldn't be.

They didn't speak of Runner very often since they didn't know where he was or even if he was alive. There'd been a few postcards from him, but they'd eventually stopped. He'd gone before the draft had been expanded to include men in Runner's age group. They didn't know if he'd joined the military or if he'd hidden out of defiance. One never knew which way Runner would turn.

Although they hoped for the best, it was entirely possible that Runner had met with disaster due to his reckless nature. Speaking his name too much would bind his spirit to the Earth instead of letting it go on to the next life if he no longer lived. Raven had decided that if Runner hadn't returned by the end of June that he and a few others would go searching for him again. Even if Runner wouldn't come home, at least they would know if he was all right.

Coming out of his depressing musings, Raven said that he and Dusty should join forces against some other card players since Dusty was skilled at gambling. It would be a good distraction. They walked across the clearing with Raven steadying Dusty when he tripped.

Tim twirled Renee around out on the Watering Hole's dance floor once she was off for the night. He was glad that she loved her new job so much. She had fun every night and she was making good tips along with a good salary. She'd informed him that she still intended to work after they were married—that was, until he was elected to congress.

He loved the way she believed in him and wanted to work together to make things better for others. There were a lot of men who didn't want a feminist for a wife, but not Tim. He wanted better opportunities for everyone, women included. He wanted the daughters he and Renee would have to be able to pursue their dreams without being discriminated against.

Their wedding was set for the end of June. They were anxious for the time to pass quickly and yet enjoyed their time together. They'd agreed on no more intimacy until they were married, neither of them wanting an eight-month baby. After having known that kind of passion, this wasn't easy, but they'd remained steadfast in their decision.

The next night, Friday, was the high school graduation and they were both proud of their brothers and Snow Song for graduating with good grades. A big graduation party was planned at the community center for all of the graduates so Jake had given her the night off to celebrate with her family.

As they danced, Tim kept glancing at the ring on her finger and smiling as he thought of the night of their engagement. He'd enjoyed the look of happy surprise on her face and the way her eyes had sparkled. He forced his thoughts away from the memory of what had occurred next between them. When he took her home and kissed her goodnight, he smiled inside as he thought that they were one day closer to their wedding.

Skip sat in between Joey and Lyla Samuels, who was also graduating. He was nervous about walking to receive his diploma because he didn't want to trip or do anything stupid. There were ten other kids graduating including Sam Wild, Moose and Katie's second child, Jeff Samuels, son of J.R. and Chloe, and Olivia Taylor, Mason and Aiyana's daughter.

While their principle, Claire Samuels, gave a speech congratulating the students on a job well done and giving them encouragement to go on to do great things, Skip's mind drifted away to the events of the past few months. He knew that Renee wanted to find her assailants and testify against them, but he wanted blood.

When they'd been little, she'd kept people from picking on him and had been his best friend until he and Sawyer had become friends. She was still his best friend, just in a different way. There were things that he wouldn't talk to anyone other than her about, not even Sawyer. He was happy that she was getting married because he wanted her to be happy, but he was sad for himself.

He knew he could still go see her whenever he wanted to and he would be over at the Dwyers' a lot since he was close friends with Joey, but it still wouldn't be the same. His attention was brought back to the present when Joey got up to go get his diploma.

Joey smiled and waved at the audience as he walked over to Claire.

She laughed at his cocky attitude and thought about how much she was going to miss him around school the next year. She loved all of their students, but as in many cases, there were those students who touched a special place in an educator's heart and Joey was one of them.

"Congratulations, Joey," she said, handing him his diploma.

"Thanks, Mrs. Samuels," he said, shaking her hand. "I'm gonna miss seeing you when I get sent to see you."

She laughed. "It's a funny thing, but I'll miss that, too."

He let her hand go and waved to the audience again, drawing laughter and loud applause before going back to his seat by Skip. The kids around him laughed, including his wife. She was called next and Joey clapped and whistled while she walked over to Claire, which made her laugh. When she came back, Joey grabbed her and kissed her, not caring who saw.

"I'm so proud of you, honey," he said.

"I'm proud of you, too," she whispered back.

When Skip's name was called, he was relieved when he made it across the stage without embarrassing himself. Claire was proud of Skip because he'd sometimes struggled in school—not scholastically, but socially. He'd been made fun of, but he'd persevered through it and had gotten good grades in spite of the days he'd missed when he'd been too angry to attend school.

All of the teachers had tried to make sure that the other students didn't ridicule Skip, but the teachers couldn't always be around. She was glad that Skip had gained the friendship of Joey and a few other boys who always stood up for him. Skip could take care of himself physically, but his temper could turn dangerous and he sometimes couldn't control it. Once, he'd beaten up one boy badly before he'd been pulled off of him.

As a result, he'd begun running away from the situation whenever someone started something with him. He didn't want to go to jail for assault so he avoided getting into that kind of trouble by walking away. Sometimes he disappeared for hours until he cooled down.

Claire shook his hand. "Justin, I'm so proud of you and I'm going to miss you."

He smiled. "I'll stop in to see you," he said.

"I look forward to it," she said.

He walked back to his seat, smiling when he heard his family and others cheer for him. He waved bashfully and sat down again. Lyla had so much family present that the auditorium was filled with noise when she went to collect her diploma. Claire proudly gave her niece the document and Lyla returned to her seat.

Dawson's school district wasn't large, but their teachers were top notch and the students' grades were generally high. Although there were only thirteen students graduating, there were many more students in the lower grades than ever before, requiring the hiring of more teachers. The school had added on two more classrooms because the other ones were too crowded.

The ceremony ended and most of the crowd moved to the community center where the celebration commenced. Switch had been right about people still getting alcohol—moonshiners were making money hand over fist selling their homemade brew. When the party ended at the public venue, many home parties went on, some of them serving homebrewed spirits.

It was also hard for the law to be enforced in private homes because the police needed a search warrant to raid a home. However, there had to be evidence of the illegal sale of alcohol before a warrant would be issued. The Dwyers were no exception in rebelling against the new law.

One day, Joe remarked about almost being out of liquor to Black Fox, telling him that he was saving what they had for Joey and Snow Song's graduation and Tim's wedding.

The chief said, "I will send someone to talk to you about this." That was all he'd been willing to say about the matter.

Watching his family and friends celebrating, Joe thought back to what had happened when Winona's husband, Brown Otter, had shown up at the house a few days later, wanting to speak privately with Joe. Since he was deaf and Joe had never caught on to Indian sign very well, Brown Otter wrote in a notepad to communicate with the mayor. Joe smiled as he thought back to that day...

"Black Fox says that you may not have enough liquor for your parties," Brown Otter wrote.

"Yeah, that's right," Joe said, nodding.

"I can help you with that. Do you have time to come with me right now?"

Joe liked the mischievous glint in Brown Otter's eyes. "Yeah. I can come now." His curiosity was too strong for him to wait.

"I brought you a pony to ride," Brown Otter told him.

"All right. Let's go."

Brown Otter had taken him far out into the woods, past the big falls above camp. They stopped at what looked like a tangle of bushes and vines. However, Brown Otter pulled some of the vines back to reveal the mouth of an old mine shaft. As Joe slid off his pony, he noticed that some of the wooden supports had been replaced. He gave Brown Otter a curious look, but the brave just smiled and motioned for him to follow.

Lighting lanterns along the way, Brown Otter stopped at a doorway several yards from the mine entrance. Opening the door, he lit another lantern and led Joe inside. Over in the far corner of the huge room stood a large homemade still. It was obvious that the room had recently been carved into the mountain, but the walls had been plastered over and whitewashed.

Joe looked at Brown Otter in disbelief. "Is that your still?" he asked, pointing first at the equipment and then at the Indian.

Brown Otter nodded and laughed at the shocked expression on Joe's face.

Joe let out a shout of laughter and clapped his hands together in glee. "I don't believe it."

Brown Otter flashed him a grin and motioned for Joe to follow him again. Farther on down the shaft, they came to another door, which was padlocked shut. He opened the door and went into another recently created room, holding his lantern aloft. Joe stared in open-mouthed wonder at the bottles of what looked like whiskey lining shelves along one wall. On the other side of the room sat several barrels of what must contain beer.

He'd been too busy looking around to notice Brown Otter pouring a sample of the moonshine. Joe absently took the glass that Brown Otter pressed into his hand. He raised it and downed the shot the way he would any other. It had a slightly different flavor than other whiskeys, but it was smoother than a lot of homemade whiskey Joe had tasted over the years.

"Damn, that's some fine moonshine, Brown Otter," Joe said, giving him the Indian sign for good. He pointed over at the barrels and signed, "What?"

Brown Otter took another cup over to one with a spout on the side and Joe watched as amber liquid flowed from it. His mouth practically watered at the sight of the beer. He took the cup and tried a sip. It was on par with many good beers.

"How long have you been doing this?" he wrote on Brown Otter's notepad.

"Six years."

Joe's eyebrows jumped up. "Six years?"

Once again, Brown Otter had Joe follow him to yet another room that contained more barrels of beer and whiskey. He noticed that dates had been painted on the oak barrels.

Brown Otter wrote, "We kept it a secret because the alcohol had to age first. I was going to start selling some to Jake once it was aged enough, but with the new law, I can't now. I had to wait for the whiskey to reach maturity. It should go a little longer, but it's not that long off that it can't be drank now. The beer is from this past fall when we harvested the hops and barley we planted. I was going to sell some privately, too, but I can't do that legally. I do not want it to go to waste."

"Me, neither," Joe wrote. "Let me think." He paced back and forth a few minutes. He'd been doing some checking into the prohibition laws, which stated that wine production was allowed for communion and other alcohol in small home-made quantities.

The amount of alcohol Brown Otter had on his hands was more than a home-made quantity, but how could they make it seem as though it wasn't?

He took the notepad again. "I need someone to translate. Let's go see Black Fox."

Brown Otter nodded and they headed back to camp.

Joe had been glad that Switch had been with the Chief at the time because his craftiness had come in handy. The plan he'd come up with was simple. If people came to camp and consumed some spirits, it was just among friends, with no money exchanging hands—at that moment. However, if people were to hand a few select people some money to give to whatever person they named from the tribe as a personal loan repayment, no one would be the wiser.

Therefore, as far as anyone knew, Brown Otter only made small batches of homemade brews, which he shared with his friends when they stopped by. Joe laughed to himself at the cleverness of his unconventional friend. That way, they wouldn't have to worry about setting up a secret establishment and risking discovery.

The location of Brown Otter's operation was still on the tribe's land, so there was no issue about the land usage. This also meant that it could be kept a secret since only a few people would take the necessary ingredients there and retrieve the alcohol. Yes, it pleased Joe greatly to be able to skirt around the law that he strongly opposed.

He drained the glass of beer he'd been drinking and then went to sing with the gang who'd come to provide music for them.

Chapter Seventeen

The day of Renee and Tim's wedding, the sky rumbled, lightning flashed, and rain descended from the heavens in torrential sheets. Renee looked out the window at the horrible weather with dismay, hoping that it would clear off by the time she had to leave for the church. She wasn't worried about superstition; she was worried about her hair.

Then she remembered all of the cowboy hats in their costume room. If she wore one of those, it would keep the rain off her hair so that it wouldn't be wet when she arrived at the church. Even with an umbrella, it could get wet if the wind blew strongly. She would pile all of her hair on top of her head and put the hat over it, thus protecting it.

She chose a white, boy-sized hat that fit her smaller head. All of the others were too big. She pulled the stampede string tight and thought that if it could keep the hat on during a stampede or other fast movement, it would keep it anchored to her head in the storm.

Hope saw her trying it on. "What on Earth are you doing?"

"Keeping my hair dry until I get to the church."

"It looks cute on you," Hope said, smiling.

Renee smiled. "Does it?"

"Yes, it does."

"Maybe I'll ask Pa if I can have it and wear it around the ranch to amuse everyone. Other women wear them, but I never thought about wearing one," Renee said.

"I'm sure he'll let you have it," Hope said.

"I'll convince him," Renee said, winking. "We should leave for the church soon. I was hoping it would slow down out there, but it doesn't look like it's going to."

"No, it doesn't," Hope responded. "I don't want my dress to get dirty, either. Or my hair to be ruined. I'll put a scarf around it."

"You look beautiful, Ma," Renee said. "No wonder Pa fell in love with you. He tells me that he's quite the charmer when he wants to be. Is that true?"

Hope eyes twinkled. "You have no idea how charming he can be."

Renee giggled. "Does he give you a certain look? The kind that makes you all warm inside?"

Hope laughed. "Why do you think I married him after only knowing him a week?"

"I guess that answers that question," Renee said, laughing. "Well, I guess we should brave the storm so we're not late."

The women went to collect the men and get underway.

An hour later, Renee was almost in tears. The storm had only gotten worse, getting them wet despite only having a short ways to walk to and from the car and using umbrellas. The strong wind had ripped one of them out of Skip's hand and he'd gotten soaked. The torrential rain and high wind had created two leaks in the church requiring a regular changing of buckets.

Maybe we should postpone the wedding, she thought. *No. Come hell or high water, I'm marrying my cowboy today!*

Tim had left for the church with Kyle and Randy in one of their Model T cars. They hadn't known that the creek about a mile from their house had overflowed its banks, flowing across the road, which was very muddy by this time. Upon seeing the washed-out road, Tim turned around and went back to the house.

"What are you going to do?" Randy asked.

"What we've done for hundreds of years: ride a horse. We can cut across camp and take the trail that leads up to the main road heading into town," Tim said. "We need to warn the rest of the house about the road. They won't be able to take a buggy, either. There's no telling how deep that water is right now."

Once they'd reached the house, Joe put a hand on Tim's shoulder. "Son, I hate to say it, but maybe we'd better postpone the weddin'. I don't want to risk everyone's safety. It ain't gettin' any better out here." A jagged streak of lighting struck the ground out in one of the pastures and they cringed at the accompanying thunder.

"Damn it!" Tim said.

"I'll call the switchboard and have whoever is on it let Mac and Renee know. She'll understand," Joe said right before another crash of thunder sounded overhead.

More than anything, Tim wanted to marry Renee that day. He didn't want to wait any longer, but the right thing to do was postpone until the next day.

"All right, Daddy," he shouted over the next rumble of thunder so Joe could hear him.

However, the electric and telephone were out because of the storm. Tim put his hat and slicker on. "I'll go let them know," he said. "I'll be fine."

His family watched him go, praying for his safety as he rode out of sight into the deluge.

—m—

When Tim reached the church, there was a brief break in the weather. He tied his horse close to the hitching post and ran into the church, where he met Matt.

"You shouldn't have come," Matt said, concerned over Tim's welfare.

"I think we're going to have to postpone. The church now has four leaks and Moose said it came over the telegraph, which is still working by some miracle, that there are more bad storms coming shortly."

As if to confirm Matt's statement, lightning lit up the windows and a horrific crack of thunder followed. Hope came upstairs and saw Tim.

"Oh, my gosh! You shouldn't have come, Tim. It's too dangerous." She fell silent as she looked out the windows.

They followed her to the side door, which she opened a little bit. The light outside had changed to a greenish color and the clouds overhead roiled.

"Everyone to the basement!" she shouted. "Downstairs now!"

The men saw the same thing and agreed with her. Tim pulled out his pocket knife and said, "I'll be right there!"

"Where are you going?" Matt shouted as Tim left the building.

Tim knew that if a twister formed while the horses were tied to the hitching posts they would be trapped by their tethers. As a horse rancher, Tim's first concern was more for his animals than himself. He ran along slashing reins and halter ropes, freeing the animals so they could run to safety.

"Ha! Get goin'!" he shouted at them to get them to move, knowing that they would be found later on or that the horses would go home once it was safe.

Most of the horses were upset as it was and took off willingly—all except for Skip's mule, Dash, who had apparently broken out of the livery stable where he was kept with the other Keller horse. He hated being away from his family and he was so strong that keeping him contained was hard when he was very determined to go somewhere. Most likely the nosy mule had seen the other equines gathered at the church and had decided to come see what was going on.

Although he wasn't an aggressive animal, Dash's ears swept back and he stamped a front foot when Tim tried to force him to move away. Tim didn't have to time to argue with the mule, so he ran around to the front door, which was closest to him now. When he went through it, he discovered that he wasn't alone. Dash pushed in right behind him, knocking Tim out of his way as he barreled inside.

"You can't be in here!" Tim said. "Get out!"

The seventeen-hands-tall mule's answer was to shake off like a huge dog, soaking Tim further. Matt and Devon had come upstairs to see if Tim had come back in and they received the same treatment from Dash.

Devon's bridesmaid dress was now sprayed with water and mud, as was her face and hair. "Dash! What are you doing in here?"

Tim and Matt tried to push him back outside, but it was impossible to move the sixteen-hundred-pound animal. When the wind howled and the rain came sideways, they gave up and ran down to the basement.

Upon hearing that Tim had arrived at the church and had agreed that they should postpone the wedding, Renee had scooted into the washroom there and changed back into her skirt and blouse. She ran over to him, embracing him.

"I'm so glad you're all right. You shouldn't have come. It's too dangerous," she said.

"I had to so you knew that I didn't get cold feet," he said, smiling.

"I wouldn't have thought any such thing. I'm just glad you're safe."

The building above them creaked and groaned and they quieted, listening in fear. When the groaning grew louder, Renee grabbed Tim's shirt collar.

"We're getting married right now, Timmy. If I'm going to die, I'm going to die as your wife!"

"Honey, it's gonna be all right. The storm will pass and we'll get married tomorrow," he said. "I want my family to be here. I don't have my best man or my tuxedo or—"

A horrendous crash overhead interrupted him, shaking the building, and Dash let out a frightened bray. Tim and Renee looked at each other, their eyes wide and frightened. They moved over to Matt.

"Marry us right now, Mac," Tim said. "We're not dying without being married."

Matt said, "You don't have rings."

Renee said, "We don't have to have them right now, do we?"

"Well, it's unorthodox, but what the heck? Everyone gather around," Matt said.

Switch came to Renee and dragged her away.

"What are you doing, Pa?" Renee asked.

"I'm walking you down the aisle," Switch said. "I'm not letting this damn storm deprive me of that."

Watching Switch walk Renee over to where Matt and Tim stood made the rest of those gathered laugh, adding a little levity to the dangerous situation. Another crash met their ears. The couple tightened their grips on each other's hands.

Matt said, "We're skipping over a lot, but Tim do you take Renee as your lawfully wedded wife, to have and to hold, to love and to cherish until death do you part?"

"I do," Tim said.

"Renee, do you take Tim to be your lawfully wedded husband, to have and to hold, to love and to cherish until death do you part?"

"I do," Renee said.

Matt had to shout to be heard over the din. "I now pronounce you man and wife! Kiss your bride!"

While the storm raged around them, a different tempest swept Tim and Renee along as they soundly kissed each other. The weather outside may have been dark and dangerous, but in their hearts and souls there was only love and light. The ceiling creaked and moaned above them. It began sagging and Matt shoved everyone into the kitchen, where the ceiling was stable. They'd all just crammed into the room when the boards gave away completely.

One of the mighty oak trees close to the church had been a victim to the storm and had fallen on the structure, smashing through the building. The weakened floor hadn't been able to hold its massive weight and the tree fell down into the basement. The group inside cowered in a corner, the men instinctively shielding the women with their bodies.

Water poured into the basement, flooding the floor.

Black Fox yelled, "We cannot stay here! It is too dangerous!"

The rest concurred and they began making their way around tree branches to the stairs that miraculously were still intact. Matt led the way up them. The sight that met his eyes caused tears to well in them. The tree filled the sanctuary and many of the pews had been crushed. His attention was diverted from it by Dash, who butted him with his head. Matt was able to move him away so that the others could get up the stairs.

The wind blew pages of hymnals around along with leaves and small branches. They had to shield their faces from the swirling debris. Matt tried to open the door to the outside, but it wouldn't budge. Several of the men tried to open it, all of them exerting their strength at once, but it still wouldn't open.

"The building must have shifted and now the door is stuck," Matt said.

"We have to get out of here!" his wife, Penny, shouted.

Skip hollered, "Get out of the way! Move back!"

In Skip's hands, Dash was always completely compliant. Skip had worked with him since he'd been a foal, forming a powerful bond. At Skip's urging, Dash quickly moved around until his rear faced the door.

"Kick!" Skip shouted. "Kick, Dash!"

The mighty mule lashed out, his powerful haunches and legs sending his hooves crashing into the door, blowing it wide open.

"Get out!" Skip told him.

Dash turned and trotted outside, braying as though bragging about what he'd just accomplished.

The twenty-odd people poured forth from the building and turned to look back at it as they were drenched by the raging storm. They gathered together, drawing comfort from their closeness as they looked upon the ruined building. As they looked on, more of the building succumbed to the combination of weight and wind and collapsed. They gazed around at each other, all of them thinking that they'd narrowly escaped severe injury or death. Other townspeople came to see the destruction and to take the shocked and drenched people to safety.

Once the storms finally subsided enough and the rain stopped, Tim went to the *Dialogue* office to see if the telephone was working again. It wasn't. He went back to the Keller home, which had only suffered a few shingles being ripped from the roof.

"Sweetheart, I have to go out to the ranch to let them know we're all ok. The telephone and electric are still out," Tim said. "I'll come back with the gang so we can help around town."

"I'll help, too," Renee said.

"Honey, you don't have to do that," Tim said.

She fixed him with a look. "How would it look for the wife of the future Congressman Dwyer to not help our town in a time of need? Besides, I have a lot of friends that I want to check on, and I can help out with anyone who's wounded."

He smiled at her. "Boy, I like the sound of that. My wife." Holding her, he said, "I'm so glad we went ahead and got married. I'm sorry our wedding got ruined in one way, but I'm not sorry we had Mac marry us. When I think what might have happened if I hadn't come when I did …"

Renee tightened her arms around his midsection. "Don't think about that. We're safe and sound. That's more than others can say."

"No wonder I love you so much."

"I'm going with you to tell your family about us getting married," Renee said.

Skip said, "Take Dash. He can hold the both of you and he's more surefooted and able to get over obstructions."

Tim nodded. "Good idea."

Renee had changed into jeans and an old blouse. "I'm ready."

Switch and Hope hugged her.

"Be careful," Hope said. "Switch and I will go to the hospital to help with incoming patients."

Skip said, "I'll start helping around town however I can."

Tim and Renee mounted Dash and made their way through the camp up to the Dwyers'. Pasture fences lay on the ground and shingles had been ripped from some of the buildings. One of their trees was down and a couple of the sunroom windows were broken. They rode up to the house and slid off Dash. Tim tied him to a hitching post and they went inside.

Most of the family was gathered in the parlor and greeted the newlyweds with relief that they were safe.

Tim put his arm around Renee and said, "We have to tell you something, and please wait to get mad until we explain it all to you."

"All right," Lacey said.

Tim said, "We're gonna need our rings, Kyle, because we had Matt marry us."

The expressions on the family's faces were filled with surprise and dismay.

Renee understood why they were disappointed about not being there for their wedding.

"Please let us explain," she said.

She and Tim told the story of their narrow escape and why they'd wanted to get married in a rush. The family understood their reasoning and were shocked by how close they'd come to being hurt or worse.

"Thank God for Dash. He might have been an accident, but I'm sure glad he was there," Tim said. "He and Skip saved us."

Kyle had gone to his room and he came back with their wedding bands, which he handed to Tim.

Joe snatched them and said, "I'm the mayor so I can do this part at least. I guess I have that power." He handed Renee's to Tim and said, "Repeat after me, Tim."

Since he'd been to so many weddings, Joe had memorized the ceremony. He guided them through the ring exchange. "I now pronounce you husband and wife … again. You may now kiss your bride … again."

Everyone smiled at his performance. Tim and Renee didn't mind repeating their kiss as their family applauded them. They were hugged and Randall said they should have a quick toast before seeing to repairs, not only at the ranch, but in town, too.

Joe and Lacey watched Tim and Renee as Kyle raised a toast to them and the love in their eyes convinced them that the young couple's choice had been the right one. They split up, some of the people working on the ranch and the others heading for town.

By the time they arrived home that night, the Dwyer clan was exhausted. The destroyed church had gotten the worst of it, but there had still been a lot to be done elsewhere in town. This sort of thing had happened a long time ago, prompting Joe's deputy mayor, Cassie Benson, to organize a disaster relief plan for the town.

Joe knew that if it hadn't been in place, dealing with the aftermath of the storm would have been much harder. They'd helped board up broken windows and Renee had patched up minor wounds and assisted in taking people to the hospital for further treatment. Cora and Lucy had fixed a meal and they heated up food for the tired workers arriving home.

After eating, Tim and Renee went to his room.

This is my home now and I'm going to be with Tim from now on. That thought filled Renee with happiness, but she also felt nervous. It was another new place she had to get used to, but she wasn't alone this time. This was what she'd been waiting for: beginning her life with Tim. And yet she didn't know what she should do. *One thing at a time. Clean up and get ready for bed.*

They had planned to stay at the Dawson Hotel overnight before leaving on their honeymoon, but that plan had been derailed by the storm. In the morning, they would take stock and decide when they wanted to leave.

Tim was also disappointed about the way things had turned out, but he was determined to make the best of the situation.

"Why don't you go ahead and use the washroom first?" he suggested.

"All right," she said.

Tim could see the tension in her shoulders and apprehension in her eyes as she gathered her things.

Going to her, he said, "This isn't how it was supposed to be, but I'm not sorry that we got married today, honey. Everything is gonna be fine because we're together now. We can get through anything together and we'll get through this."

She put her hands over his where they rested on either side of her neck. "You're right. We've gotten through much worse than this. All that matters to me is being with you."

He gave her a brief kiss and then she went to clean up. While she was gone, Tim went to the linen closet and got out fresh sheets. Cora had taught all of the kids how to make beds, saying that there was no reason they couldn't do it once they were older. He put the new sheets on the bed and then smiled as he put his boots back on.

Quickly, he ran outside and cut some of the new roses from one of the bushes and hurried back inside to the kitchen. He knew where the vases were kept and put the roses in one and hurried back to their room, running past Edwina, who was coming out of the parlor. She saw the flowers and guessed what he was up to.

Grinning, she went to her and Randall's quarters, where she began gathering up some fragrant candles.

"What are you doing, love?" Randall asked.

Edwina's green eyes smiled. "I'm helping our newlyweds have a nice wedding night."

Randall immediately rose from the sofa. "You take those. I'll get a bottle of the champagne we were saving for their reception."

She kissed him and said, "You are such a smart man. I'm so glad I married you."

Randall said, "I'm smart for marrying you, m'dear. Let's hurry."

When Renee came back to their room, she was surprised at the transformation in it. The freshly made bed was turned down and rose petals had been sprinkled on it. A vase of the beautiful flowers sat on Tim's dresser. Several lit candles were placed around the room and a champagne bucket sat on a nightstand along with two champagne flutes.

She smiled at Tim's thoughtfulness in doing something so special for her. She wondered where he was and then decided that she should get her surprise ready for him since he wasn't there. When she was done, she sat down on the bed and reclined back on her hands to wait for her groom.

Tim entered their room and leaned against the closed door as he took in the beautiful, alluring woman sitting on the bed. He'd never seen anything like what she wore and he found it more provocative than any other lingerie.

She'd modified a pair of boy's underwear, slitting them up the side and adding pink lace along the bottom. They molded to her thighs and flattered her curvy hips. She'd done something similar to the button-down shirt, replacing the normal buttons with little pink flowers and cutting it lower to reveal a hint of cleavage. Her hair was pulled into a high chignon and pearl earrings dangled from her earlobes. A burning hunger for her filled Tim as he took in her lovely form.

Renee was equally fascinated by him in a men's silk robe with his hair freshly washed and combed. It was such a contrast from the way he normally dressed that it looked exotic and enticing.

"You are the most gorgeous, beautiful woman I've ever seen; I'm so proud to be married to you," he said, coming towards her.

"Thank you," she said, excited by his smoky gaze. "You're the handsomest, most virile man I've ever seen."

Tim stepped over to his closet and reached inside it, surprising her by pulling out a guitar.

"You play?"

"Yeah. I sing, too, but I can't do it in front of lot of people. Daddy keeps trying to get me to play with them at the bar, but I just can't," he said, sitting down on a chair.

"But you're going to play for me?"

He nodded, smiling bashfully. "I'm gonna try."

Renee sat up against the headboard as he settled the guitar on his lap and strummed a little to warm up. The love song he played for her was incredibly sweet, but the tender way he sang it made it more so. His voice was in the low tenor/high baritone range and very smooth. His fingers moved with confidence over the strings and his bashfulness disappeared as he looked at Renee. Through the song, he told her what was in his heart, using the music to convey all she meant to him.

When he finished, tears glittered in her eyes. She clapped softly and motioned for him to come to her as she stood up. Tim set the guitar down and embraced her.

"That was so beautiful. Thank you."

"You're welcome. I love you, honey, and there's nothing I won't do to make you happy," he said, cupping her face in his hands.

"And I'll do anything to make you happy," she said, untying his robe. "You're overdressed, Timmy."

Smiling, he let it slide down over his shoulders. "I can take care of that," he said, letting it fall to the floor.

Her dark, desire-filled eyes captured his gaze and he couldn't look away as he lowered his head to kiss her. Her lips were warm and soft and Tim thought he would go crazy with wanting her. Tim suddenly discovered that Renee's shyness regarding making love with him had gone. He thrilled to the way her hands traveled over him and the way she kissed him passionately.

He returned the favor and was rewarded by her moan of need. His control broke and he quickly divested her of her unconventional, fascinating lingerie. She let out a little squeal as he suddenly picked her up and laid her on the bed. The candlelight illuminated her eyes as he lay down beside her, and the love reflected in them touched a place deep inside that he hadn't known existed.

"Make love with me, Timmy," she whispered. "I need you and I love you so much. I never thought it would be possible to love someone the way I do you. I belong to you now."

He moved a hand to her hair, releasing it from the chignon and delving his fingers into the silky mass. Fisting his hand in it, he tugged a little. "That's right. You're mine now and I'm yours. I belong to you forever, Renee, and I'm going to show you how much I love you."

His aggressive attitude excited her and she slid her arms around his neck, pulling him closer so she could kiss him. Soon they were wrapped up in each other, giving their hearts, souls, and bodies to each other as only two people in love can.

It was a connection unlike anything they'd ever experienced and as they drifted down from the pinnacle together, an unbreakable bond formed, making them confident in their commitment to one another. That night, as Renee lay in Tim's arms, no nightmares tortured her. His presence chased away the frightening images and kept them at bay until the sun came up.

Chapter Eighteen

Raven hadn't intended for so many people to go with him to South Dakota to look for Runner and he hadn't planned on going on horseback. His father had talked him into making the trek over the trail that way instead of taking a train or driving.

"This will be the last time I will get to make such a journey, Raven," Black Fox said. "I know the way and I would like to experience this with you and some others. There will be more of us to search and secure game as we go."

Looking into Black Fox's eyes, Raven had responded to the longing in them and he hadn't been able refuse such a request. He thought back to his boyhood when they had traveled south every year and had attended the Sun Dances. He missed those times and he'd grown excited at the prospect of sharing a journey like that again with his father.

"Yes, Father. I would like that very much," Raven had said, grinning.

Now, a few days after Tim and Renee's wedding, he looked around at the large search party gathered and smiled. His Uncle Owl, Mike, Uncle Striking Snake, Aunt Squirrel, Reckless, Marcus' son, Eric, Jonathan, Skip, Dino, and Hailey were all assembled and ready to go.

Raven hadn't minded including some of the younger set since they'd never had a chance to go on a trip like this. Skip had packed Dash down with the majority of the gear they would need since the mule could haul huge loads.

Mules are hardier animals than horses, requiring less feed, able to withstand heat much better, and able to go long distances without water. Rarely do they overeat or drink too much, which would result in foundering if they did. They also have a higher sense of self-preservation and think about things more before deciding to do them. While some of their training is similar to horse training, they require more patience, but once they learn something, they rarely forget it.

Skip understood all of this about Dash and his hard work and love in training his mule was evident in the way he obeyed Skip. The boy constantly fussed over and talked to Dash, which made the mule willing to do what was asked of him. Raven was glad to have such an animal along on the trip.

They were seen off by their tribe and other family and friends who wished them good luck and promised to pray for a safe, successful trip. As they rode out of camp, the group's spirits were high and they looked forward to the journey with excitement and optimism.

Renee delivered drinks to a table and went back to the bar with empty glasses. She'd thought she would be upset about not going on a honeymoon right away, but she found that she didn't need that to be happy with Tim. They'd decided to postpone it until next spring and she was perfectly content in her new life with Tim.

During the day while he was working, she always had something to occupy herself with until she went to work at four Wednesday through Sunday. Tim often came to the Watering Hole, dancing with her on her breaks and following her home after the night was over. Jake closed the bar around eleven since it seemed that most of the crowd was gone by then. Without being able to serve alcohol, the clientele had changed somewhat and most of them went home earlier since they had to work in the morning. On her days off, Renee volunteered at the Reading Center and she and Tim had dinner with her family on those nights.

When the time for the rodeo came, she helped organize some of the events. Joe and Cassie were impressed with her ideas and by the responsible way she carried out her duties. The attendance was down a little from the previous year, but the influx of business was still substantial and everyone profited.

That Thursday, Renee was on her way back to the bar to have Andy fill an order when she heard a coughing laugh. She froze for a moment and then forced herself to casually look around as though checking for empty glasses. At a table off to her right, two men sat together; one stocky with a reddish beard, the other taller and leaner.

Renee saw the scar at the base of the bearded man's throat. A rush of fear and nausea hit her as horrible images assailed her mind. Somehow, she managed to make it to the bar. Andy was alarmed by her pale complexion and terror filled eyes.

"What's wrong?" he asked, concern in his green eyes.

"I need someone to go give this note to my father," Renee said. "Don't ask why. Just please send someone quickly. It's very important. Please?"

Andy took the note and said, "Sure. I'll go myself."

"Thank you," Renee said.

Andy let Jake know he was leaving and took off. Renee went back to waiting tables, keeping an eye on the two men, who watched the dancing. She also noticed that they watched her, which made it hard to act normally. Two men came into the barroom that now doubled as a club house and walked past her.

One of them winked at her—she recognized him as Mitch. He was dressed in jeans and an old button-down blue shirt. However, he now sported a short beard and mustache. The man with him was his son, Shawn, who wore a cowboy hat and mustache. He also wore older clothing to blend in.

They went back to the pool room and Renee waited five minutes before executing her part of the plan. She took a deep breath. *You can do this, Renee. It's time to exact your revenge and to put them where they can't harm any more women. You're an actress so put on the performance of your life!*

Going to their table, she smiled at them. "Hello, gentlemen. Are you enjoying the entertainment?"

The taller one just gave her a surprised stare, but the shorter one said, "Uh, sure. There's always good music here."

His was the rough, gravelly voice from the night of her rape. She worked hard to keep her smile in place. "Yes, they do such a good job, don't they? Would you handsome fellas like more to drink?" She gave them a sultry look. "It's very hot out. I thought you might be parched."

She watched with hate as the taller man's eyes heated with hunger.

"Sure," he said. "Another sarsaparilla for us both."

"I'll be right back," she said, moving off.

While she waited for Jake to give her the drinks, she composed herself again. Renee used her hate for the men to fuel her determination to get through what was about to happen. She returned to their table and put their drinks down.

"Would you like to play some free pool?" she asked, winking. "I have some pull and they'll let you slide if I ask them to."

"Why would you do that?" the shorter man asked.

"When I meet fine men like yourselves, I always like to show my appreciation. It's time for my break. I can't make any wagers, of course, but I'm certain that I can beat you," she said, smiling slyly.

The taller one said, "You're on."

She led them back to the poolroom, her heart pounding. She kept reminding herself that Mitch and Shawn would keep her safe. Entering the poolroom, she took down a pool stick and chalked it up while they did the same thing.

"What are your names, boys?" she asked.

The taller man said, "I'm Logan and this is Bret."

"Nice to meet you boys in a proper setting this time," she said.

Logan frowned. "What do you mean?"

Renee smiled at him. "Don't play dumb, Logan. I know who you are and you know who I am, too."

Bret smiled. "So you remember the good time we gave you, huh?"

"No, what I remember is that you beat the crap out of me and violated me," Renee said. "That's what I remember."

Logan said, "Shut up, Bret." He advanced on her, but she stood her ground. "If I were you, I'd be careful what you say, little lady."

"Or what?" she asked. "You'll give me more of the same?"

Bret sent her a malice-filled smile. "That can be arranged. We know where you live."

"Shut your mouth, Bret!" Logan snapped.

"What's the matter, Logan? Don't you want people to know what a weak little man you are? How it took two of you to rape a poor defenseless woman? How much of a coward you are?"

Logan's hand shot out, gripping her hard around the throat. "I'll show you that I'm all man, just like I did that night."

He felt something grip his ankle and then his foot was yanked out from underneath him. He fell down and found himself facing Mitch, whose eyes shone with fury. The sheriff socked him in the jaw twice before rolling out from under the table. While he'd been dealing with Logan, Shawn had come out from behind the opened poolroom door and had subdued Bret by grabbing a fistful of his hair and slamming his face down onto one of the pool tables.

Both men handcuffed their prisoner. Renee strode up to them, her eyes blazing with rage.

"I'm going to tell everyone who will listen what you did to me and I'm going to testify in court. I'll help put your asses in the clink where you'll never be able to hurt anyone ever again. You picked on the wrong woman, you worthless, pathetic excuses for men. And since I'm Joe Dwyer's daughter-in-law, my word will carry a lot of weight."

Logan blanched. "You married a Dwyer boy?"

"That's right. I guess you hadn't heard. Like I said, you picked on the wrong woman," she said and spat in their faces.

Mitch grinned. "You did good, Renee. We'll meet you back at the office."

He and Shawn took the deviants out of the bar while people watched and murmured to themselves. Andy came into the poolroom shortly thereafter to find Renee sitting on a chair, sobbing. He went over to her, crouching by her.

"Renee, are you hurt?"

She shook her head as he put an arm around her.

Tim came in the bar and greeted Jake. "Is everything all right? I saw Mitch and Shawn hauling a couple of guys out of here."

Jake knew that whatever had happened had something to do with Renee. "I think Renee's in the poolroom. That's all I know."

Alarm shot through Tim and he raced back to the poolroom, spying Renee and Andy.

"Renee? What happened?" he asked.

Andy rose and left the room to give them some privacy.

Renee cried harder when she saw Tim and he knelt and wrapped his arms around her.

"Shh. It's ok now. I'm here," he crooned to her.

His familiar embrace made her feel safe again and she raised her head from his shoulder.

"We got them, Tim. We got the men who raped me," she said.

Tim's eyes widened in shock. "They were here? That was them with Mitch and Shawn?"

"Yes."

As she explained the situation to him, anger gripped Tim, but he pushed it down. It wasn't the right time to talk about it.

"I have to go to the sheriff's office to give my statement," she said.

"I'll take you. You shouldn't drive right now," Tim said, getting off his knees.

He kept an arm around her shoulders as they left the bar and got in his car.

As Tim listened to Renee's story as they sat at the sheriff's office, his anger grew hotter. It was a good thing that Rick Westlake was helping at the office because Tim had tried to get back to the cells twice. They'd had to subdue him and keep him away from there.

Once Renee was finished, they quickly left the office before Tim grew even more agitated. He was silent on the way home, his jaw working and his hands clenching on the steering wheel. Renee let him alone, knowing that he was close to exploding.

"Go on in the house," he said tersely once he'd pulled into the garage.

"Tim—"

"Please, Renee. Go on in the house."

She exited the car and walked up to the house. Back in the garage, Tim pounded repeatedly on the steering wheel until his hands were sore and his breathing ragged. Even though he was furious with her, he hadn't wanted to do that in Renee's presence, afraid that he'd scare her. Calmer, he went to the house, going straight for the whiskey on the mantel in the parlor and pouring a generous amount into a glass. He gulped it down and poured more while Cora watched from where she sat on the sofa.

"Does this have anything to do with Renee walking through here cryin'?" she asked. "I couldn't get her to talk to me."

Tim had been so caught up in his thoughts that he hadn't noticed her. "Yeah. I don't wanna talk about it, either. I'm too mad."

"Hmm. And that whiskey is gonna do you more good than talking to me?"

He let out a derisive snort and shook his head. "Talking. I wish my wife had talked to me."

Cora pursed her lips. "I can't help you if I don't know what you're talkin' about, Timmy."

"I'm talkin' about tellin' your spouse things that are really important instead of keeping them to yourself," Tim said. "Goodnight, Cora." He tossed back his second drink and then took his glass to the kitchen.

Renee changed for bed and sat down on a chair, trying to soothe her nerves before Tim arrived. When he did, her stomach started to hurt because she could almost feel his anger.

He sat on the bed and looked at her. "How could you do that?"

Renee said, "I had to help catch them, Tim. I needed to put them in jail so they can't hurt me or any other woman. I doubt that I'm the only one they've assaulted."

Tim nodded. "I understand, and I'm proud of you for having the courage to face them. That's not what I'm talking about."

Her brows drew together as confusion filled her. "Then what *are* you talking about?"

"Renee, haven't I been there for you through everything? Given you unconditional love, support, and comfort?"

She moved over to the bed and tried to take his hand, but he pulled away from her. "Of course you have, and I'll never be able to repay you."

His face tightened. "I don't want repayment. Don't you trust me?"

Her eyes grew bigger. "I trust you implicitly, Tim. Completely."

"Then how could you not tell me about this plan? How could you not include me in something so important? I'm your husband."

The hurt in his eyes made her heart ache. "I'm so sorry."

"If you couldn't tell me about this, what else are you withholding from me?" He got up and paced back and forth.

"Nothing, I swear," she said.

"Are you sure about that? I know how sneaky you can be," Tim said. "You could be hiding something else."

His belligerent attitude pricked her temper. "Excuse me? Are you saying that I'm a liar?"

"Maybe not a liar, but you're good at keeping secrets and formulating crafty plans."

Her hands fisted in the comforter. "Tell me something, Tim. If you had known about the plan, would you have let me do it?"

He crossed his arms over his chest and looked away from her.

"Exactly. You would have tried to do something to prevent me from helping to catch them. You would have let them go free by doing so. So, no, I didn't tell you—or anyone outside of my father and the sheriff's department," Renee said.

His eyes that were usually filled with warmth when he looked at her stared coldly at her. "You didn't even give me a chance."

She stood up, trembling with rage. "You have no idea what it's like to be tackled to the floor, repeatedly hit, each blow harder than the last. You don't know the shame, the terror I felt as those men ripped open my nightgown and did detestable, degrading things to me. Until you know that kind of fear, that kind of pain and sheer horror, you have no right to judge the way I'm dealing with this.

"I did what I had to so they were caught and if that meant not telling anyone about our plan, then so be it. I wasn't going to let anything stand in the way of doing something about what happened to me and showing them that I wasn't going to let them ruin my life by being a cowering, weak woman. I wouldn't give them that satisfaction, that power. I'm sorry that I hurt you, but I did what I had to."

Tim shook with rage at the images her words brought to mind and his heart filled with hurt that she'd felt that he wouldn't have supported her decision.

"I'm going to sleep in one of the other bedrooms," he said stiffly.

He quickly left the room, leaving Renee to stare after him in disbelief and sadness. The stress of the evening got to her and she needed an outlet. After dressing, she went to the garage and cranked their Model T to life. As she drove away from the estate, tears ran down her face. She went to Sawyer and Devon's house, knowing that she could talk to them.

She was relieved to see lamplight in their parlor windows. She knocked on their door and Devon answered it. Devon saw that Renee was upset.

"Come in. Are you all right?" she asked.

"Not really. Will you lend me an ear?"

"Of course. Come sit in the parlor," Devon said.

Renee looked around the homey room. She liked the oak paneling, pretty pictures, and comfortable furniture. A large blue-and-white braided rug that matched the curtains covered much of the hardwood floor.

She greeted Sawyer, who relaxed in one of the wingback chairs that sat in a corner.

"Hi," he said, his brown eyes roaming over her. "You don't look so good. What happened?"

Devon had put the kettle on and now she settled on the sofa by Renee.

Renee's tale poured forth, her words coming fast as she related the events of that night. "And now, Tim thinks that I don't trust him and that there are other things that I haven't told him. I've told him that there's nothing else that I've kept from him. I trust him completely, but I was afraid that if he knew about this plan that he would keep me from doing it. It would have been out of concern and love, but he might have kept me from carrying it out."

Devon nodded. "He might have. Tim loves you so much that he'd do anything to keep you safe. But you don't know that for sure."

Sawyer said, "One thing that we've learned since we've been married is that we tell each other everything. If we have a difference of opinion we work through it. Withholding things will just lead to problems, just like it did with you and Tim."

"I *have* told him everything. Just not that," Renee said.

Devon said, "I think the problem is that you kept such an important thing from him."

Renee put her head in her hands. "You're right. It was an important thing. I let my need for revenge consume me and I didn't consider his feelings. I should have talked to him. Now what do I do? He doesn't want to talk to me."

Sawyer chuckled. "I've been where you are and it's not fun. Let him cool down and then swallow your pride and apologize. That's what I did with Devon and it eventually got through to her."

Devon said, "But so did Renee. You made me see that I was also letting pride get in the way of my happiness with Sawyer and I'm grateful to you for that."

Renee gave her a wan smile. "I'm glad I could help."

Devon fixed them all some tea and she and Sawyer tried to bolster Renee's spirits. They also praised her for being so brave in assisting with the rapists' capture. By the time she left, she felt a little better. It didn't last, however. Their bedroom was still empty. Renee changed for bed and slid under the covers, but she didn't sleep. Instead, she watched the hands of their windup clock go around until her eyelids finally closed near morning.

—m—

The next morning, Tim came into their room as Renee was dressing. He ignored the desire that shot through him at the sight of her and gathered some clothes.

"Tim, I know that you're upset with me, and I'm so sorry that I hurt you. I never meant to."

"Well, you did, and I'm so angry with you," he said. "I can't believe that you shut me out like that." The pain in his heart made his chest ache. "I'm your husband, but you couldn't trust me."

"Tim, please try to understand—"

He collected his clothes with angry movements. "I can't talk about this. I have to get to work."

"What about breakfast?" she asked.

"I'm not hungry." He gave her a sad glance and left the room.

Renee forced back her tears as she finished dressing. She put on her actress persona and went out to breakfast, smiling as she sat down at the table. Several of the family could see past her façade, however, and they knew that Tim had slept in a different room. Joe thought it was a shame that they were fighting, and he surmised that it had something to do with the capture of those men, but he didn't know the details of what had happened.

Everyone loved Renee and enjoyed her witty banter. She fit in well with the family and Joe and Lacey were happy with the addition of their new daughter-in-law. The kids often asked her to read them stories because she acted out the parts as though putting on a play. She played tag and hide-and-seek with them. Renee enjoyed being around them and looked forward to having children with Tim.

As she ate her breakfast, she didn't taste the food. In her state of distress, it had no flavor and she didn't see the beauty of the sunshine or hear the lilting melody of the birds. She went about her day, but there was no joy in her heart. Normally, she enjoyed her job, but that day it was hard to find any enthusiasm for going to work.

Although she was pleasant and attentive to the customers, her anguish showed in her eyes and Jake and Andy were concerned about her. Renee left work as soon as she could that night, hoping that Tim would be receptive to her. However, she found their room empty and knew that he wouldn't be sleeping there that night.

Chapter Nineteen

Over the next week, Renee repeatedly tried to talk to Tim without success. He'd closed himself off behind a wall of anger and pain. The more he rebuffed her, the hotter Renee's anger burned. Eventually she stopped trying.

Joey hated seeing his big brother in pain and he hated seeing Renee so sad. Going to bed one night, he put his arms around Snow Song and asked, "How'd you like to help get Tim and Renee back together?"

She snuggled closer. "I'd love to. What did you have in mind?"

"Well, Renee says that every time she tries to talk to him, he brushes her off and leaves. We're gonna make it so that he can't do that and he has to listen to her," Joey said. "See what you think of this idea..."

Tim finished cleaning a stall and came out of it. Joey stood at the end of the corridor of stalls.

"Hey, Timmy. Can you come help me in the storeroom a second?" he called out.

"Yeah. I'll be right there," Tim said, moving his wheelbarrow to the next stall he was going to clean.

He found Joey in the storeroom. "What do you need?"

Joey moved up to him and said, "Now!"

Tim hadn't seen Kyle and Sonny Grayson near the doorway inside. The three men jumped Tim, forcing him into a chair they'd put in the middle of the room.

"What the heck are you guys doing?" Tim asked, struggling against them.

He was no match for the other three strong men and they tied him securely to the chair.

"Why are you doing this?" he demanded.

"Because you're being an idiot," Kyle said.

They heard Snow Song approaching with Renee.

"You have to see these kittens. They're so cute. One of them reminds me of Romeo," she said, leading Renee into the storeroom.

Renee looked around at the men and saw Tim tied to the chair, his face a mask of fury.

Joey took hold of her arms and moved her away from the door. "Just stand there a moment."

The others ran from the room, slammed the door shut, and locked it from the outside.

Renee ran to the door, pounding on it. "Let us out! Hey! Open the door!"

"Not until you talk this out!" Joey hollered back.

"Open this door now, Jr.!" There was no response. She let out a noise of frustration and then turned to face Tim.

He glared at her and Renee became angry.

"Don't look at me like that, like I'm some enemy," she said. "I'm your wife and I deserve a chance to explain things to you, but you won't talk to me. Do you want the rest of our marriage to be like this?"

Tim's jaw clenched. "No."

"Then talk to me. I want to work this out," she said approaching him. "I miss you. I miss our life together and I miss sleeping with you at night."

The way she walked accentuated her shapely figure in her skirt and blouse and he knew she was doing it on purpose. He'd discovered that

Renee could be a seductress and she excited him like no other woman. Even as angry as he was he wanted her with a ferocious intensity.

Renee silently thanked her friends for giving her the opportunity to set things right between them. She surprised Tim by coming right to him and straddling his lap. Her weight settled on him and his hunger grew stronger. She smelled so good and he longed to touch her.

"Tim, I've apologized for hurting you several times. I'll keep doing it if that's what it takes to get through to you, but I never tried to hurt you. I'm sorry for keeping you in the dark. I let my desire to get revenge blind me to how you would feel when you learned about our plan. It was wrong of me and I'll always regret it. Can't you please forgive me?"

It was hard to think when she was running her hands over his shoulders and her sweet lips were only inches from his, but he gathered his wits. "I'm your husband—the person you're supposed to trust and count on the most. I can tell you with complete certainty that while I would have hated you trying to pull off a dangerous stunt like that, that I would have understood and helped you with it.

"But you didn't give me that opportunity. And part of why I've been so mad is selfish. I would've liked to have had a part in bringing those asses to justice! I would've liked just a few minutes with them to make them sorry for what they did to you." Tears stung the backs of his eyes. "It's my job to protect you and I didn't get to be there for you! I didn't get to see your bravery and the looks on those guys' faces when you caught them! I want to be part of your crazy schemes and share everything with you. Don't you want that, too?"

She suddenly understood. She'd robbed him of the chance to help get revenge upon the men who'd hurt her so badly. "Of course, I do. I want to share everything with you, too. I swear that I'm not keeping anything else from you and that I'll never have any secrets from you again. I promise you that."

Tim read the sincerity in her eyes and saw that she was genuinely contrite. He'd learned when Renee was acting and when she wasn't.

"Please forgive me?"

He couldn't stay angry in the face of her honest plea. "You swear that you'll never have any secrets from me again?"

She smiled as hope surged through her. "I swear it."

A smile tugged at the corners of his mouth. "Ok. I forgive you."

She embraced him, tears trickling from her eyes. "Thank you so much. I love you and I would never hurt you on purpose, Timmy. You *are* the person I trust most and I need you so much. You make me so happy, and I want to make you happy, too."

His dark eyes were once again filled with that familiar warmth that she loved so much. "You do make me happy. Happier than I ever thought possible. I knew after Devon's wedding that I wanted you for my own and I set out to get you."

She ran her fingers through his hair. "And you did get me. I'm so glad that you captured my heart. No other man would have stood by me the way you have. No other man could have loved me the way you did. And I would never have wanted any other man to make love to me for the first time. You showed me how beautiful making love is supposed to be and you've shown me every time since. My heart, my soul, my body—all of it belongs to you, Tim, and it always will."

Tim responded urgently to her when she kissed him and his arms strained at the ropes that bound him as his need to touch her grew. He growled against her mouth as her kiss grew more aggressive. Quick as a flash, she had his shirt unbuttoned and parted. Her talented hands ran over his muscular chest, fanning his desire into a white-hot flame.

He tore his lips from hers. "For God's sake, Renee! Quit torturing me and untie me!"

She loved the way his broad chest rose and fell with his ragged breathing. "My, my, but you look so tasty." She lightly bit him and pressed kisses along his collarbone.

"Renee, untie me!"

Chuckling, Renee slid off him and released his ropes. She squealed in surprise and excitement as he crushed her against him and gave her a demanding kiss before dragging her to the floor with him. Then he got up, ran to the storeroom door, and turned the inside lock so even if it was unlocked it from the outside, no one could get in.

He came back and they laughed as they tried to get each other's clothes off. Finally they accomplished it and embraced, releasing all of their pent-up passion for each other. There in the dimly lit storeroom, they reconnected, once again giving themselves to the person they loved most in the world.

Epilogue

Renee kept her promise to Tim and included him in all areas of her life from then on. Tim had learned that closing himself off to discussing problems between them only hurt the both of them and was a big waste of time. He wanted the time he spent with Renee to be happy, not filled with anger and sorrow. They grew closer every day, their bond of love stronger than ever.

When the time came for Logan and Bret's trials, Renee testified, telling her story to the jury with confidence, even when tears rolled down her face. Although she was scared, she took strength from all of her family and friends who were there, but most of all from her loving husband.

Marcus testified on her behalf, looking each member of the jury in the eye as he told them about the horrific injuries inflicted upon her by the defendants. He was a sensitive person and the memory of Renee's battered body brought tears to his eyes. It was noticed that more than one man on the jury wiped away a tear.

Between their testimony and that of Mitch and Shawn Taylor, the jury was outraged and found the two rapists guilty after only a fifteen-minute deliberation. The judge in the case was also furious and gave each of them twenty years in prison.

After giving an exclusive interview to J.R. Samuels of the *Dialogue*,

Renee sought refuge at home, wanting only peace and quiet. She and Tim walked out by one of the pastures, holding hands.

"Have I told you lately how proud of you I am?" he asked her, tucking her hand into the crook of his elbow.

"You might have mentioned it a time or two, but I don't mind hearing it again," she said, smiling.

"Well, Mrs. Dwyer, I'm so very proud of you and you're going to make a fantastic congressman's wife," he said.

"Thank you," she said. "I want to help other women like me, Tim. I want them to know that they have someone who believes in them and who's there to support them like I do. I don't know what I'd have done if I hadn't had all of you. I probably wouldn't have pressed charges, or if had, I might not have gotten very far."

They stopped and leaned on a fence, looking at the group of mares and foals in the pasture. Tim put his arm around her. "What did you have in mind?"

"I'm not sure yet," Renee said.

"We'll figure it out together, just like we will everything else." He looked at the sky. "We need rain real bad. It's a good thing that Brown Otter figured out how to irrigate their crops or they'd be ruined by the time September comes if we don't get rain."

"I know. This drought is terrible. The last rain we had was that horrible storm on our wedding day."

Tim laughed. "Well, at least it'll make for a good story someday." He sobered. "Renee, you know, if I get elected in a few years—"

"*When* you get elected, Timmy. When."

"Right. When I get elected, we'll have to live in Washington part of the time. Does that bother you?" he asked.

She faced him. "Tim, I'd follow you anywhere, anytime. As long as you don't mind me speaking my mind—nicely, of course—I have nothing against living there. I believe in everything you stand for and I know you can do Montana, and a lot of other people, so much good."

He put his hands on her shoulders. "And so will you. You and I together will be unbeatable, Renee. Between my bullheadedness when I get something in my mind and your scheming, there's not much we won't be able to get done. Thank you for believing in me."

"Thank you for believing in me," Renee said. "And I'll always believe in you, no matter what."

He kissed her and said, "I'm glad I had the good sense to marry you."

"It seems like we're both pretty smart," she said. "I think we should go swimming and cool off. What do you think?"

"That's a great idea. Let's get our suits." Tim grinned. "On second thought, who needs suits?"

Renee gave him a coy look. "Are you telling me that you want to go skinny dipping?"

"I knew you were a smart woman," he said, grabbing her hand. "I know a good place to go."

"I'll just bet you do."

They ran to the trail leading down to camp, laughing together in the bright sunshine. They'd faced some terrible, dark storms, but together they'd found their way through, back into the light. The waters ahead would be choppy sometimes, but by remembering to rely on each other, they would withstand the ocean of uncertainty.

Joe and Lacey sat on the veranda, watching Tim and Renee run off into the woods.

"Do you think Timmy will get elected someday?" Joe asked her.

Lacey nodded. "I do. He'd be great in office, too. He has the right temperament for it, and he's very intelligent."

"Sounds like my wife," Joe said.

She smiled. "He is a lot like me. He looks like me and he's slightly quieter than Joey and Emily, but he's a lot like you, too. He's got your instincts about a lot of things, especially business. And he has your dimple."

She pinched Joe's cheek a little and he laughed. "Thanks, darlin'. Renee will help get him in, you watch. She's a firecracker and she's stronger than most people realize. She's not a woman you want to mess with. She shoulda been a spy."

Lacey laughed, but said, "Yes, I think that job would have suited her."

"It sure has been interesting watching them all grow up, hasn't it?"

"Especially our oldest and our youngest so far. Devon was easy to raise, and Kyle's somewhere in the middle. He's even quieter than Devon sometimes," Lacey said. "He's always been like that."

"Yeah, but he writes great letters. He says all sorts of things in his letters that I've never heard him say out loud, but he's not exactly shy. He likes goin' out and doing stuff with his brothers and he's been out with a couple of girls. Hey, I wonder if he met any pretty French nurses across the sea," Joe said.

Lacey grinned. "You're such a romantic."

"I am," Joe agreed. "I like seein' everyone happy. He's our only single kid now. Listen to me trying to marry him off."

Lacey said, "He'll find someone when the time is right."

While they moved on to talk about the newly built church, inside the house, Hunter ran up to Sawyer, who'd come to see if Devon was done for the day.

"Hi, Uncle Sawyer," he said, sitting Percy, the kids' ferret, on the floor.

"Hi, buddy."

Sawyer laughed when Percy climbed up him to perch on his shoulder and root through his hair. "That tickles, Percy. Knock it off." He got a hold of the critter, handing him back to Hunter. "There you go."

"Thanks," Hunter said, his hazel eyes smiling. "Look at Percy's belly." He held the ferret up and showed Sawyer Percy's rather sizeable girth.

"Looks like he's been eating good."

"He's a she and she's having babies after a while. Uncle Rick says so. I guess when he brought Percy's friend Snarky to visit that's what happened. They made some babies. I'm not supposed to tell, but I think you know how to keep a secret, right?" Hunter asked.

Sawyer almost burst into laughter, but he kept a straight face. "That's right. I won't tell another soul. Am I the only one who knows?"

Hunter said, "Just us kids know. Uncle Rick says that it's a surprise for Pappy and that we shouldn't spoil it."

"So why are you telling me?"

"Because I know I can trust you," Hunter said. "And besides, it's killin' me not to tell someone. I better put Percy away. See ya."

Sawyer laughed as Hunter ran off, picturing Joe's stunned reaction to having a litter of ferrets in the house. It might give him a heart attack. He was still grinning when he went to find Devon.

Raven watched his father at the head of the line of the search party and smiled for the hundredth time since they'd left Dawson as fond memories of his youth washed over him. He remembered the first raid he'd ever gone on and the first adult hunt that Black Fox had taken him on. How proud he'd been when he'd helped bring down a bison bull. Black Fox's praise had meant more to him than the prize of the bull's horns since his arrow had been the one to actually pierce the bull's heart.

He remembered hearing some of the older men criticize Black Fox for being too tenderhearted. Raven had challenged those men, telling them that his father was more of a man than they could ever hope to be. They'd been surprised that he would speak to them like that, but they hadn't rebuked Raven.

What those men hadn't understood was that Black Fox drew his strength from the tender heart that beat inside the body of a great warrior and chief. If it weren't for his kindness and consideration, he wouldn't have protected his people so effectively nor worked so hard to make sure their tribe didn't starve.

Speaking of tenderhearted, he thought. His view of Black Fox was obscured by Skip, who had nimbly stood up on Dash's broad back. The boy shielded his eyes from the sun to look around from his higher vantage point. He was looking for game, which had gotten scarce over the last couple of days. His vigilance had paid off as they'd traveled; he'd alerted them to deer, rabbits, and even some pheasant.

Raven smiled as Skip crouched a little and hopped up in the air, coming down to land squarely on Dash's back again. The mule was used to his master's behavior and took no notice of it. The way Skip hopped up and down like that reminded Raven of a prairie dog. He was glad to have Skip along. He was useful for such things and his freakish sense of balance allowed him to take risks that the others couldn't or wouldn't.

Skip was good with weapons and was a good hunter. He was also entertaining and helped break up the monotony of the trip with his antics. Raven wished Dusty could have shared the journey, but he'd declined, knowing that he would have been more of a liability than a help. Hailey was another matter, however. She rode ahead of Raven, her back straight, her manner alert.

He would have loved to see her in battle in France. He was certain that she'd fought as fiercely as she did everything else. Although, he did notice a little more tenderness in her where Art was concerned. He liked the man whom he was certain would be his son-in-law one day. Art didn't take crap from Hailey and he made her laugh, both of which Raven felt she needed.

Then his mind turned towards his youngest boy and he scanned the low hills they were entering. *Where are you, my son? Do you still live or does your spirit walk the next life with your grandmother? I pray that Wakan Tanka has blessed you and that you are healthy and happy. I have many questions for you, even though I think I know some of the answers. Can you feel us coming? I hope you can. If so, come to us. I am angry with you, but more than that, I love you and I want to see you again. I want to take you home to see the rest of your family. Your mother's heart cries for you every day. Hear* my *heart, my son, and come to us.*

Gazing up at the sun, Raven prayed to Wakan Tanka, the Great Creator, to help their search be fruitful and to keep them safe until they returned home.

The End … Almost …

Bonus:

The Courtship of Emily and Bobby

Episode Two
August 24, 1903

Sitting outside the school at lunchtime, Emily tried not to think about the fact that she wasn't sitting with her beau, Bobby Night Sky. It was the first day of the school year, and Emily normally liked school. However, it wasn't the same without Bobby, who'd graduated the previous year.

Her friend, Kimmi Robertson, sat down on Emily's bench and noticed her downcast expression.

"Emily, you'll see him after school," she said.

Emily smiled a little. "I know that I'm being silly, but I can't help it. Just wait until Zach graduates. You'll know what it's like then."

Kimmi said, "I'm sure it'll be hard."

"Too bad our men aren't the same age as us," Emily said. "I'm proud of Bobby for stickin' it out. He was so happy to be done with school since he hated it so much."

"And now he has his own business," Kimmi said. "He's a smart one."

Emily looked in the direction of Bobby's Bath House, the endeavor Bobby had started right after his graduation. He'd gotten the idea for the business venture during the rodeo the previous July when a few people had asked him where they could go to clean up. He knew that a lot of towns had public bath houses and he'd decided that Dawson should have one, too.

He'd found a spot down near the stream that ran down by Thompson's Feed Mill to put the business. He'd been saving his money from his job working for a carpentry outfit and once he'd had enough for the lumber, his buddies and family had helped him build it.

Then he'd bought five large tubs, two big eight-plate wood stoves and a bunch of stock pots in which to boil water. Owl and Hannah, his parents, had given him a secondhand washer, and he'd also had to purchase a huge amount of towels. Rick Westlake made and sold a wide variety of soaps and Bobby had struck a deal with him for a continuous supply of them.

Although he hadn't liked school, he'd learned some accounting and business principles, and he'd shown some business savvy. Between the advertisements he'd put in the *Dialogue* and all of the word of mouth people had done on his behalf, news of his enterprise had quickly gotten around town. He charged a dollar for a bath and he'd been happy when twenty people had shown up for baths on the first day he'd been in business.

Emily knew he wasn't far from her and she pictured him washing towels and filling tubs with hot water. He often worked shirtless since he usually got his clothes wet and it was so hot in the kitchen/laundry room of the building. She stopped in mid-chew of her sandwich as she saw those glorious, light bronze muscles of his in her mind. He was bound to be sweaty from the steam and she felt the familiar hunger for him that he brought out in her.

She was so caught up in her daydream that when a bouquet of flowers was suddenly thrust in front of her, she yelped in surprise and dropped her sandwich on the ground.

A hand descended on her shoulder. She recognized Bobby's touch and his chuckle sounded in her ear.

"Well, I didn't mean to make you do that," he said as she turned to face him. "Sorry."

"I don't care. I'm just so happy to see you," she said, wrapping her arms around his neck as he crouched before her.

His amber eyes smiled into hers. "I'm happy to see you, too. It's strange not to be coming to school with you. I thought I'd come see you quick in my lunch break. Butch is watching the bath house for me."

Emily said, "I'm so glad that you did." Not caring who saw, she pressed a brief kiss to his sensual lips. "I'll come down when school is over."

"No, you won't. You know you're supposed to go home to do your work. Don't get grounded," Bobby said, looking into her beautiful hazel eyes.

"I'll only stay for a little bit."

He chuckled. "Your 'little bit' will turn into an hour. I know you, remember? Go home and I'll see you tonight."

She grinned and ran a hand up under his long, black hair. It was slightly damp and he smelled of soap and fresh sweat. The two scents made a pleasant aroma. "Do you promise to come see me?"

"I said I would, didn't I? When have you ever known me to break a promise?"

"Never," she said. "All right. I'll go home."

He kissed her cheek and handed her the flowers. "I'll see you then. Behave."

She smiled as he stood up. "See ya." Watching him lope across the street, she said, "Isn't he the handsomest man you've ever seen?" She sniffed the flowers in her hand. "And so thoughtful and sweet."

Kimmi laughed. "You're so funny. When are you getting married?"

"He hasn't asked me yet, but we've talked about it plenty. One of these days, he'll make it official. I can be patient. I have to graduate first and I was thinking about going to college, so I wouldn't want to get married until after that," she said.

Kimmi's brown eyes were filled with doubt. "You can hardly stand being away from Bobby now. How are you going to be able to go away to college?"

Emily sighed. "I know, but I wanna do something a little different for a while. Don't get me wrong. I love my family and Dawson, but I don't want to settle down and start havin' babies right away. I want that someday, just not now."

"Have you told Bobby that yet?" Kimmi asked.

"No," Emily said.

"I don't think he's going to take that well."

Emily sighed. "I know. That's why I haven't told him yet."

Kimmi said, "If I were you, I'd tell him sooner rather than later so he can get used to the idea."

Nodding, Emily said, "I'm workin' up the nerve. We better get back so we're not late."

Kimmi gathered her things and followed Emily back into the school.

That evening as Emily and Bobby sat dangling their legs into the bathing pool upriver from the Lakota camp, Bobby took her hand and kissed it.

"Why are you so quiet? What's on your mind?" he asked.

She looked at him, wondering how she could bear to leave him, and yet she felt that going to college was something she needed to do.

Turning his strong hand over, she traced his life line and the other creases on his palm with a finger. "This is my last year of school and I've been thinking about what I'm going to do once I graduate."

"Did you decide on anything?" A tingle of warning ran up his spine.

"Well, I'd like to go to college. The University of North Dakota admits women and has a really good business curriculum," she said, keeping her eyes on his hand.

We've never really talked about it, but I wondered if she might want to go to college. It's different hearing her say it, though. I don't want her to leave me! And I don't want to go to college. How will I live without seeing her every day? Bobby took a few moments to compose himself, then said, "And you're worried about me being mad, aren't you?"

She nodded and he saw a tear fall onto his hand. Bobby's heart cried whenever she did.

"Hey, I'm not mad. I figured that you'd want to go to college. You're too smart not to. That school isn't so far away that I couldn't come see you now and again," he said. "The train runs right through Grand Forks, so it won't be hard to get to you. I can have someone drop me off in Williston and I'll just take the train from there. And you'll come home in the summers."

"You're not angry?" She was finally able to look at him.

He brushed away her tears. "No. I'm going to miss you like crazy, but I'm not mad. I love you, and when you really love someone, you don't stand in the way of their dreams. If this is what you want, then I'll support you."

She embraced him tightly. "You're always on my side."

"And I always will be."

Laying her head on his shoulder, Emily said, "It's only for two years."

Only? It sounds like a lifetime to me. "I can wait two years."

Drawing back, Emily met his gaze. "Are you sure?"

"Yeah, I'm sure." He dragged her over onto his lap. "I'd wait as long as it took. I might hate it, but I'd do it."

She cocked her head at him. "Why do you love me? I argue with you, I get you in trouble, and I don't know when to shut up."

Bobby smiled. "Yeah, but you have a lot of good qualities, too."

"Like what?"

He frowned in concentration and then confusion. "You're right. What am I thinking?"

Emily let out a scream as he pushed her off his legs into the bathing pool. She went under and came up to hear Bobby laughing.

"Bobcat! You're a dead man! You just wait until I get out of here! This was a new skirt, too, damn it!" she hollered, her face red with the force of her anger. "I can't get out of here with this thing on."

Bobby was weak with laughter as she floundered around in the water. Emily quickly reached behind her, undid her skirt, and pulled her legs up out of it. She flung it out of the water before lifting herself out of the pool, making a beeline for Bobby, who sprinted away. In only her blouse and pantalets, Emily sped after Bobby into the camp.

Marcus sat at the central fire with Claire and Black Fox as the young couple raced by them.

"Huh. I wonder what that's all about," Marcus said.

Claire laughed. "It must have something to do with Emily being soaked. Bobby must have dunked her."

Black Fox chuckled and took a bite of his brownie as he looked after Bobby and Emily.

Marcus said, "Wow! Look at Emily go. Wait. Where's she going?"

The girl had veered out of sight, making the trio curious about where she'd gone. They soon had their answer when she reappeared in their line of sight galloping full-out on one of their Indian ponies. They erupted in laughter at her ingenuity as she bore down swiftly on Bobby.

There was a collective gasp as they saw Emily lean off the horse as she closed in on her prey and fall on Bobby when she was near enough. They went down together on the grass near the entrance of the trail leading to Emily's home. After they rolled over several times, Emily ended up on top. She threw up her arms and let out a victory yell while Bobby laughed.

Black Fox started to laugh and a piece of the brownie got stuck in his throat, making him cough. Marcus thumped his back.

"Easy, brother. I keep telling you all those desserts are gonna kill you. Seems like I might be onto something."

Black Fox swatted his hand away. "Stop! I am fine."

They watched Bobby pick Emily up, sling her across his shoulder, and disappear into the trees.

Claire giggled. "I wonder what they're going to say up there about Emily coming home only half-dressed."

Black Fox grinned. "I will find out tomorrow and let you know."

—~—

Lacey sat out on the veranda with Randall and Timmy. The thirteen-year-old boy strummed on his guitar and hummed along.

He stopped. "What the hell?"

Randall sat close enough to smack the back of his head. "Watch your language, young man."

Timmy absently rubbed his head as they watched Bobby come toward them carrying Emily across the huge lawn. Lacey got up when she saw that Emily was scantily clad and that what clothes she did have on were dirty and grass stained.

Lacey started down off the veranda. "Emily! Are you all right?"

Emily grinned as Bobby put her down. "I'm fine, Mama. I just went for an unexpected swim, thanks to a certain someone," she said, elbowing Bobby.

He laughed. "I'm sorry. I couldn't resist."

Randall cleared his throat, drawing the brave's attention. "Timmy, go inside."

Timmy scowled up at him. "Why? I didn't do anything wrong."

"I know, but go inside anyway," Randall said.

"But, I wanna see—"

"Timothy!"

Randall's tone of voice told Timmy he meant business. He stomped off into the house, grumbling to himself.

Lacey said, "Emily, go to your room and put on some clothes, please."

"Mama, we were just playing around."

Lacey pointed and now Emily went inside while arguing with her mother, who followed her.

"Now, Bobcat, perhaps you can tell me why you brought Miss Emily home without her skirt." Randall said.

Bobby sobered at the stern look on Randall's face. "Uh, well, it was a joke."

"Removing a girl's skirt is rarely a joke," Randall said.

"I didn't take it off. She did," Bobby said, rushing to clear up the confusion. "I just pushed her into the water."

Randall arched an eyebrow. "And why would you push a fully clothed person into the water?"

"Because it was funny. I mean, we were talking and I teased her and then pushed her into the water," Bobby said. He knew he was digging himself into a deeper hole.

"Mmm hmm. So you agitated her and then pushed her in the river."

"No! Not the river! The bathing pool," Bobby said. "We were sitting there talking and she asked me why I loved her when she argues with me and gets me in trouble and stuff like that. And I said she has other good qualities. She wanted to know what they were. I said I didn't know and pushed her into the bathing pool."

Randall crossed his arms over his chest and cocked his head. "You're not helping your cause."

Bobby's shoulders sagged. "It's one of those things that you have to be there to understand."

"Apparently so. When did her skirt come off?"

"She couldn't get out of the pool, so she took it off," Bobby said.

"So, not only did you push her in, but you also wouldn't help her out."

Bobby made a frustrated noise. "It wasn't like that. I couldn't stop laughing to help her, so she took it off and got out. That's when she chased me across camp and jumped off a horse to get back at me."

Randall hid a smile. "That's certainly an unusual type of revenge."

"Well, she couldn't catch me, so she took one of the Indian ponies and chased me on it. When she caught up to me, she jumped off it and landed on top of me."

"Oh, I see. Well, that certainly clears that up," Randall said. "You truly love her, don't you?"

Bobby smiled. "Yeah."

"And wouldn't you agree that she's a lot of fun?"

His smile widened. "Yeah."

"And very beautiful?"

"Yeah."

"Especially without her skirt."

"Yeah." Bobby's eyes bugged out. "No! That's not what I meant! She's just as beautiful with it on. I mean, I wasn't trying to get her out of her skirt."

Randall's control slipped and he let out a loud laugh over Bobby's discomfort while Bobby stood uncertainly before him.

"Go home, Bobby," Randall said, still laughing. "But no more bringing her home half-dressed."

"Yes, sir," Bobby said, jogging back towards camp. *I can't win. If Emily is involved, I'm gonna get in trouble.* Then he started laughing to himself, thinking that any trouble he got into over Emily was worth it just to be with her. Nothing was ever dull with her around and he wouldn't change her for anything.

Randall watched him go as Joe came outside.

"Why did Emily come home with only half of her clothes on and looking like a drowned rat?" he asked.

Randall snickered. "It involves the bathing pool and jumping off horses."

"What? What are you talkin' about?"

Randall sat back down on a chaise lounge. "I'll explain it to you if you go get us a drink."

Joe looked at the sunroom and opened his mouth.

"No, no! Chet is off duty," Randall said. "*You* go get it."

Joe rolled his eyes, but did as he'd been told.

Randall grinned to himself. "People think that the rich people are the ones in charge, but they're wrong. It's the butler. Forget mama; if the butler ain't happy, ain't nobody happy." He chuckled to himself as Joe returned and handed him a tumbler of scotch.

Joe sat down. "Ok, now what happened?"

"Well, you see..."

—~—

Thank you for reading and supporting my book and I hope you enjoyed it.

Please will you do me a favor and review "After The Storm" so I'll know whether you liked it or not, it would be very much appreciated, thank you.

Connect With Linda

Visit my website at **www.lindabridey.com** to view my other books and to sign up to my mailing list so that you are notified about my new releases.

Linda's Other Books

Dawson Chronicles Series

Mistletoe Mayhem
(Dawson Chronicles Book 1)
After The Storm
(Dawson Chronicles Book 2)

Echo Canyon Brides Series

Montana Rescue
(Echo Canyon brides Book 1)
Montana Bargain
(Echo Canyon brides Book 2)
Montana Adventure
(Echo Canyon brides Book 3)
Montana Luck
(Echo Canyon brides Book 4)
Montana Fire
(Echo Canyon brides Book 5)
Montana Hearts
(Echo Canyon brides Book 6)
Montana Hearts
(Echo Canyon brides Book 7)
Montana Orphan
(Echo Canyon brides Book 8)
Montana Surprise
(Echo Canyon brides Book 9)
Montana Miracle
(Echo Canyon brides Book 10)

Montana Mail Order Brides Series

Westward Winds
(Montana Mail Order brides Book 1)
Westward Dance
(Montana Mail Order brides Book 2)
Westward Bound
(Montana Mail Order brides Book 3)

Westward Destiny (Montana Mail Order brides Book 4)

Westward Fortune (Montana Mail Order brides Book 5)

Westward Justice (Montana Mail Order brides Book 6)

Westward Dreams (Montana Mail Order brides Book 7)

Westward Holiday (Montana Mail Order brides Book 8)

Westward Sunrise (Montana Mail Order brides Book 9)

Westward Moon (Montana Mail Order brides Book 10)

Westward Christmas (Montana Mail Order brides Book 11)

Westward Visions (Montana Mail Order brides Book 12)

Westward Secrets (Montana Mail Order brides Book 13)

Westward Changes (Montana Mail Order brides Book 14)

Westward Heartbeat (Montana Mail Order brides Book 15)

Westward Joy (Montana Mail Order brides Book 16)

Westward Courage (Montana Mail Order brides Book 17)

Westward Spirit (Montana Mail Order brides Book 18)

Westward Fate (Montana Mail Order brides Book 19)

Westward Hope (Montana Mail Order brides Book 20)

Westward Wild (Montana Mail Order brides Book 21)

Westward Sight (Montana Mail Order brides Book 22)

Westward Horizons (Montana Mail Order brides Book 23)

Cast of Characters

Tim Dwyer-son of Joe and Lacey Dwyer

Renee Keller- Switch and Hope Keller's daughter

Switch and Hope Keller

Skip Keller-Renee's younger brother

Jethro Keller-Renee's older brother

Sawyer Samuels-owns the Shutter Shoppe

Devon Samuels-Sawyer's wife

Dr. Marcus Samuels-Head doctor at Dawson Community Hospital

Dr. Mike Samuels-Marcus' nephew

Chief Black Fox

Raven Dwyer and Zoe Dwyer-Hailey and Dusty's parents

Dusty Dwyer- Raven's son

Hailey Dwyer- Raven's daughter

Joe and Lacey Dwyer

Joey and Snow Song Dwyer

Kyle Dwyer-Son of Joe and Lacey Dwyer

Art Perrone- Kyle's buddy from the war

Minx-Reckless' sister

Emily Night Sky-Joe and Lacey's daughter

Jasmine Night Sky-Bobby and Emily's daughter

Hunter Night Sky- Jasmine's younger brother

Brown Otter- Black Fox's son-in-law

Matt "Mac" Mackenzie

Randy Cooper-son of Chester and Letty Cooper

Randall and Edwina Cranston

Cora Ambrose-Joe and Lacey's cook and friend

Jake Henderson

Andy Henderson-Jake's son

Mitch Taylor

Shawn Taylor

Dash- Skip's draft mule

About Linda Bridey

Linda Bridey lives in New Mexico with her three dogs; a German shepherd, chocolate Labrador retriever, and a black Pug. She became fascinated with Montana and decided to combine that fascination with her fictional romance writing. Linda chose to write about mail-order-brides because of the bravery of these women who left everything and everyone to take a trek into the unknown. The Westward series books are her first publications.

Made in the USA
Coppell, TX
23 February 2021